THEY KNEW TOO MUCH

Francis Durbridge

WILLIAMS & WHITING

Copyright © Serial Productions

This edition published in 2023 by Williams & Whiting

All rights reserved

This script is fully protected under the copyright laws of the British Commonwealth of Nations, the United States of America, and all countries of the Berne and Universal Copyright Convention. All rights including Stage, Motion Picture, Radio, Television, Public Reading and the right to translate into foreign languages are strictly reserved. No part of this publication may be lawfully reproduced in any form or by any means such as photocopying, typescript, manuscript, audio or video recording or digitally or electronically or be transmitted or stored in a retrieval system without the prior written permission of the copyright owners.

Applications for performance or other rights should be made to The Agency, 24 Pottery Lane, London W11 4LZ.

Cover design by Timo Schroeder

9781915887368

Williams & Whiting (Publishers)

15 Chestnut Grove, Hurstpierpoint,

West Sussex, BN6 9SS

Titles by Francis Durbridge published by Williams & Whiting
1 The Scarf – tv serial
2 Paul Temple and the Curzon Case – radio serial
3 La Boutique – radio serial
4 The Broken Horseshoe – tv serial
5 Three Plays for Radio Volume 1
6 Send for Paul Temple – radio serial
7 A Time of Day – tv serial
8 Death Comes to The Hibiscus – stage play
   The Essential Heart – radio play
   (writing as Nicholas Vane)
9 Send for Paul Temple – stage play
10 The Teckman Biography – tv serial
11 Paul Temple and Steve – radio serial
12 Twenty Minutes From Rome – a teleplay
13 Portrait of Alison – tv serial
14 Paul Temple: Two Plays for Radio Volume 1
15 Three Plays for Radio Volume 2
16 The Other Man – tv serial
17 Paul Temple and the Spencer Affair – radio serial
18 Step In The Dark - film script
19 My Friend Charles – tv serial
20 A Case For Paul Temple – radio serial
21 Murder In The Media – more rediscovered serials and stories
22 The Desperate People – tv serial
23 Paul Temple: Two Plays For Television
24 And Anthony Sherwood Laughed – radio series
25 The World of Tim Frazer – tv serial
26 Paul Temple Intervenes – radio serial
27 Passport To Danger – radio serial
28 Bat Out of Hell – tv serial
29 Send For Paul Temple Again – radio serial

30 Mr Hartington Died Tomorrow – radio serial
31 A Man Called Harry Brent – tv serial
32 Paul Temple and the Gregory Affair – radio serial
33 The Female of the Species (contains The Girl at the Hibiscus and Introducing Gail Carlton) – radio series
34 The Doll – tv serial
35 Paul Temple and the Sullivan Mystery – radio serial
36 Five Minute Mysteries (contains Michael Starr Investigates and The Memoirs of Andre d'Arnell) – radio series
37 Melissa – tv serial
38 Paul Temple and the Madison Mystery – radio serial
39 Farewell Leicester Square – radio serial
40 A Game of Murder – tv serial
41 Paul Temple and the Vandyke Affair – radio serial
42 The Man From Washington – radio serial
43 Breakaway – The Family Affair – tv serial
44 Paul Temple and the Jonathan Mystery – radio serial
45 Johnny Washington Esquire – radio series
46 Breakaway – The Local Affair – tv serial
47 Paul Temple and the Gilbert Case – radio serial
48 Cocktails and Crime (An anthology of the lighter side of Francis Durbridge)
49 Tim Frazer and the Salinger Affair – tv serial
50 Paul Temple and the Lawrence Affair – radio serial
51 One Man To Another – a novel
52 Tim Frazer and the Melynfforest Mystery – tv serial
53 News of Paul Temple – radio serial
54 Operation Diplomat – tv serial
55 Paul Temple and the Conrad Case – radio serial
56 The Passenger – tv serial
57 Paul Temple and the Margo Mystery – radio serial
58 Paul Temple and the Geneva Mystery – radio serial

59 The Knife – tv serial
60 Paul Temple and the Alex Affair – radio serial
61 Kind Regards From Mr Brix – magazine serial
62 Paul Temple and the Canterbury Case - film script
63 The Yellow Windmill - magazine serial (extended version)
64 Paul Temple: Two Plays for Radio Volume 2 (contains Send for Paul Temple and News of Paul Temple)

Murder At The Weekend – the rediscovered newspaper serials and short stories

Also published by Williams & Whiting:
Francis Durbridge : The Complete Guide
By Melvyn Barnes

Titles by Francis Durbridge to be published by Williams & Whiting
A Case For Sexton Blake – radio serial

For more information about Francis Durbridge please visit:
www.francisdurbridgepresents.com

INTRODUCTION

This novel by Francis Durbridge appeared as *Sie wussten zu viel* (*They Knew Too Much*), which was a ten-part serial in the German magazine *Bild und Funk* in 1963. It was a new, expanded and rather different version of Durbridge's earlier newspaper serial *The Face of Carol West*, which had been published in the *News of the World* in eight parts from 9 August to 27 September 1959. The original serial *The Face of Carol West* has been reprinted for the first time in the volume *Murder at the Weekend* (Williams & Whiting, 2020), but Durbridge completely revised this 1959 story before it reached the German magazine in 1963. Most of the character names were changed, new characters and plotlines were introduced, and even the denouement and ultimate solution were new.

But firstly, for anyone to whom Durbridge's name is unfamiliar, some background information might be helpful. Francis Henry Durbridge (1912-98) was the most popular writer of mystery thrillers for BBC radio and television from the 1930s to the 1970s, after which he enjoyed a successful career as a stage dramatist with plays such as *Suddenly at Home, Murder with Love* and *House Guest*. In the 1930s his name frequently recurred on BBC radio, with an output including comedies and dramatic plays, children's stories, musical libretti and short sketches, but in 1938 he established himself as a crime writer in particular. This was several months before his twenty-sixth birthday, when the BBC Midland Region broadcast his serial *Send for Paul Temple* and the listening public submitted over 7,000 requests for more.

The result was that he rapidly became one of the foremost writers of radio thrillers, and Durbridge's dream team of novelist/detective Paul Temple and his wife Steve was thoroughly launched – with the 1938 *Paul Temple and the Front Page Men* followed by another twenty-six Paul Temple mysteries until 1968 of which seven were new productions of earlier cases. Durbridge's radio serials also acquired a massive European following, with translated versions broadcast in the Netherlands from 1939, Germany from 1949, Italy from 1953 and Denmark from 1954. And in the UK, such was Temple's appeal that he even became a comic strip hero in newspapers for a lengthy daily run from 1950 to 1971.

The Paul Temple mysteries in the mid-twentieth century vied in popularity with the exploits of other noteworthy radio detectives - including Dick Barton (by Edward J. Mason), Philip Odell (by Lester Powell), Dr. Morelle (by Ernest Dudley), P.C. 49 (by Alan Stranks) and Ambrose West (by Philip Levene). But always a new Paul Temple radio serial was a significant event, and in addition it might come as a surprise to many fans to learn that in the 1940s alone Durbridge also created radio detectives called Anthony Sherwood (1940), Johnny Cordell (1941), Amanda Smith (1941), Gail Carlton (1943), Michael Starr (1944), André d'Arnell (1944) and Johnny Washington (1949), and he even wrote a radio serial featuring the legendary Sexton Blake (1940).

Then in 1952, while continuing to write for radio, Durbridge embarked on a long sequence of BBC television serials that achieved enormous viewing figures until 1980. Although his reputation from 1938 onwards had rested on the regular radio exploits of the Temples, it was his parallel television career from the 1950s that firmly established his name. Indeed he ruled the roost on television for nearly thirty years – beginning with *The Broken Horseshoe* in 1952 and continuing with such titles as *Portrait of Alison, My Friend Charles, The Scarf, The World of Tim Frazer, Melissa* and *Bat out of Hell*. His complex plots and cliff-hanger endings attracted enormous viewing figures, and he introduced one-off protagonists rather than simply transferring Paul Temple to television.

In the UK Durbridge's appeal on the small screen was unrivalled, with the result that for all his serials from 1960 (beginning with *The World of Tim Frazer*) the BBC gave him the unprecedented accolade of the "Francis Durbridge Presents" screen credit before the title sequence of each episode. And in Europe his television serials proved phenomenally popular, just as his radio serials had done – beginning in Germany with *Der Andere / The Other Man* (1959), in Sweden with *Halsduken / The Scarf* (1962), in Finland with *Huivi / The Scarf* (1962), in Italy with *La Sciarpa / The Scarf* (1963), in France with *L'écharpe / The Scarf* (1966) and in Poland with *Szal / The Scarf* (1970).

Many of Durbridge's radio and television serials were novelised and frequently reprinted, numerous Paul Temple radio serials have been marketed as CDs, and his television serials from *The Desperate People* (1963) to *Breakaway* (1980) were all released in 2016 as DVDs. There were also nine cinema films in the 1940s and 1950s derived from Durbridge's radio and television serials, which much later became available on DVDs – *Send for Paul Temple, Calling Paul Temple, Paul Temple's Triumph, Paul Temple Returns, The Broken Horseshoe, Operation Diplomat, The Teckman Mystery, Portrait of Alison* and *The Vicious Circle*.

Francis Durbridge died on 11 April 1998 in Barnes, a leafy area outside London that had been his home and the milieu that had become so familiar in his plots. Radio and television stations in Germany were particularly glowing in their obituaries, describing his serials as unforgettable masterpieces and recalling the days when Durbridge cliffhangers resulted in deserted German streets because a huge majority of the population stayed at home, glued to their radios and television sets. It was not surprising that commentators bestowed on him the sobriquet *Straßenfeger* – the so-called street sweeper, who compelled his listeners and viewers to abandon such activities as theatres, cinemas, bars, restaurants, leisure centres, sports, public transport and even the meetings of legislative assemblies.

There can be no doubt that Francis Durbridge was an international icon of popular culture who deserves to be remembered.

Melvyn Barnes
Author of *Francis Durbridge: The Complete Guide*
(Williams & Whiting, 2018)

They Knew Too Much

CHAPTER ONE

The Telephone Number

Victor Merton winced. His hand had hit something while diving into the water. It was soft and cold! Quick as a flash he shot upwards into the air, trying to penetrate the iridescent green water with narrowed eyes. For a moment he stared in disbelief and then he took a deep breath. He dived again, grabbed the object and pulled it to the surface. One look was enough. One look at the dripping hair, the pale face and the bare shoulders in which no more blood pulsated. The woman was dead.

Merton gritted his teeth. Damn that something like this had to happen here! Whenever the weather permitted, he did his swimming exercises early in the morning. There'd never before been any inconvenience. Why now, he thought? He turned his head and looked over towards the bungalows. Sure enough, on the terrace, old Cooper was sitting at breakfast, as he did first thing every morning. He looked up – now there was nothing else Merton could do. With three or four powerful strokes, Merton reached the step ladder of the pool, dragging the woman behind him in a rescue grip. She hung limply in his arms. Merton turned and grabbed the ladder with his left hand while his feet sought a foothold on one of the steps.

He gave a jerk. Merton had climbed another step and another rung. There was just one more to go. Merton gasped. He was athletic and tough but such a feat of strength wasn't required of him every day. The more he pulled the lifeless body out of the water, the heavier it became. Finally, Merton could see over the edge of the pool. On the terrace stood old Cooper who had jumped up. He was staring, watching what was going on. Julia, the very pretty Hungarian girl, was also there. She'd brought Cooper the morning papers. Merton saw his opportunity. He pulled himself up a little higher and shouted at the top of his voice: "Julia! Julia!" The papers fluttered to the ground and the girl ran towards the pool. Old Cooper ran after her. Arriving at the ladder, Julia dropped to her knees and with both hands she grabbed the woman's shoulders and pulled her towards her. Merton felt the support and was thankful for it. With a final effort, he rolled the woman's body over the edge of the pool. Then he climbed the step ladder. Cooper, who was now also poolside, looked silently at the woman lying there in her dripping evening dress. Then he looked at Merton. He'd already regained his composure. "Julia," he said, "we need to call the police!"

***

When the phone rang, Christian was still sitting at breakfast. He put down the knife, reached for the receiver and gave his number.

"Who am I speaking to?" he heard the man on the other end of the line ask. He didn't know the voice. Whoever it was had to wait until he'd swallowed a mouthful of toast. Only then did he get an answer.

"This is Stiller. Christian Stiller."

The caller seemed taken aback.

"Not Superintendent Stiller from Scotland Yard?"

"That's right. That's me. Do you mind telling me who you are and what you want!"

The reply came meekly.

"Certainly, sir. This is Detective Sergeant Ingram of the Belhampton Criminal Investigation Department. If I had known that Scotland Yard was already involved..."

Christian interrupted him curtly. "Wait a minute, DS Ingram, what are you talking about? And why you are calling me on my private number?"

The other stumbled.

"What? This is your private number? You're talking on your home line?" His voice became official. "If it is, sir, I must ask you to join us at Belhampton at once, if you would. I'd like you to assist us in solving a – a strange case."

"Good Lord, man, what on earth are you talking about? If you want Scotland Yard involvement, you must apply to them through the proper channels and not to me directly. You should know that!"

"It's not a question of the Yard, sir. Not yet. It's a question of you personally. I'm asking you to come – for your own sake..."

The detective sergeant wasn't prepared to say any more over the phone. He clearly knew how to arouse Stiller's curiosity. Christian didn't finish his breakfast. He called the Yard immediately and then drove to the police station in Belhampton. An officer showed him to Sergeant Ingram's office.

He greeted him politely. "I hope I haven't put you to too much trouble, sir. But you'll admit in a moment that the matter is rather strange. Please, do take a seat."

Christian sat down impatiently. The sergeant was twenty years older than he, but if he didn't finally come to the point, there'd be trouble.

"Well, sir," the sergeant said leisurely, "it was like this: three hours ago we were called to a place called The High Dive. I don't know if you know it?"

"Yes, I know it. A sort of well-tended hospitality thing just outside of London?"

"That's right, sir. Guests stay in bungalows and it has a swimming pool. It puts on music for afternoon tea and dancing in the evening, that sort of thing. It's only accessible by road."

"And what's happened there?" Christian interrupted him.

"They've pulled a girl out of the swimming pool this morning. She was dead."

"Was it suicide?"

The sergeant shook his head thoughtfully. "Only the doctor who conducts the postmortem on her can determine that exactly. But if you ask me – I don't believe it was suicide. Why would a girl who is completely unknown to anyone out there – and I've asked everyone – drown herself in the pool of the High Dive? And how did she get there? On foot? I don't think so somehow."

Christian drummed his fingers nervously on the arm of his chair. "I still don't understand what I ..."

"Well, sir, we found the dead woman's handbag. I fished it out of the water. It's all pretty normal stuff. Lipstick, comb and so on. And a notebook."

He reached into a drawer, pulled out a packet and unwrapped it. "Here on the third page, where the owner's name is entered, it says CAROL WEST, 8 DORCHESTER CLOSE, ST. JOHN'S WOOD, N.W. 8. The writing's still clearly legible. Oh, and look, sir, down here where the address book part is, there's only one phone number."

He pushed the notebook towards Christian.

"Ken. 9856," the Superintendent read. "Kensington ninety-eight fifty-six." His own telephone number!

***

Christian Stiller shivered as he entered the cold room of the morgue. It wasn't just the cold he felt in his light summer suit. It was the rows of bare stone gurneys with the silent figures on them and the pale white sheets with which they were covered. It was the pervasive smell of disinfectants. And the indifference of the attendants. He would never get used to it.

His companion carelessly pulled aside a sheet. "That's her."

Christian looked at the dead woman. He didn't hear the attendant shuffling away across the stone tiles. He concentrated on the face in front of him.

She had been young. And pretty. In her mid-twenties at the most. That wasn't an age to die. The sharp lines from her nose down had surely been dug by death. They weren't necessarily signs of premature disappointment and bitterness.

The mouth still showed traces of lipstick. The curved eyebrows, the delicate nose, the long light blonde hair that was darkened at the roots. He'd been sure that he would recognise the dead woman. She'd known him. She must have done. She had his telephone number in her book. So he must have met her at some point.

But he couldn't remember her.

Yet his memory for people was one of his strengths. He never forgot a face. That was one of the reasons why he was Scotland Yard's youngest Superintendent. He'd done three years as a policeman in Coventry, two in Birmingham with the CID, then two years as a detective sergeant with Scotland Yard's fraud squad and finally four years as a detective inspector – that was all.

His second strength was his thoroughness. But even that was of no use to him here. He systematically went through the series of women he'd met in London. Society ladies and criminals, secretaries and prostitutes, shop assistants, sportswomen, barmaids – the lot of them.

He shook his head reluctantly. No, he couldn't remember ever having seen this girl. Nor did he know the name. Carol West – that was easy enough to remember. He wouldn't have forgotten it. Still, something kept playing on his mind. Not the dead woman herself. He was sure now that he didn't know her. But she reminded him of someone he did know. She resembled someone. It was only a tiny resemblance for sure, or he would be able to recall it. Almost gently, he covered the dead woman again.

Fifteen minutes later he stopped outside number eight Dorchester Close, St John's Wood. A woman opened the door. She was about forty-five years old, stately and well-groomed. She wore a silk house coat with a floral pattern that was a little too colourful.

Christian introduced himself. At the same time he felt a wave of relief. His memory might have failed him earlier. But he recognised this woman all right.

"Aren't you Mary Kenton?" he asked.

The woman looked at him in surprise. "I was." She brushed a strand of hair from her forehead. "I'm not in the theatre any more. I quit when I got married. Fredericks is my name now. My husband died two years ago."

"You can guess what I've come for?"

"About Miss West? Someone was here earlier."

Christian nodded. "Yes, I've now taken over the case."

Mary Fredericks invited the Superintendent in.

"Would you be kind enough to tell me what you know about Carol West?"

"Gladly. But it's not much, I'm afraid. I put an ad in the paper about three months ago. I'd never rented before. But the room was empty, and I was lonely in this big, rambling house, too."

"I see," Christian said. "She had a job, of course?"

"Oh, yes. She was a secretary at Apex Insurance in Cannon Street. She was very quiet, poor thing. I had hoped she would keep me company for a bit. But she could hardly be made to talk. Sometimes she would lock herself in her room for hours."

"Didn't you wonder when she didn't come home last night?"

"Not at all," said Mary Fredericks. "She often stayed away for two or three days at a time. Said she had to go away on business."

"May I see her room?"

"Of course," she said and led him upstairs. The room was strangely impersonal. "It's like a hotel room that's rarely used," he thought. There was a small stack of books on a table. But nothing else. No flowers, no pictures. "May I use the phone?" he asked.

Mrs Fredericks nodded. Her sense of drama was obviously awakened. She listened intently as the Superintendent spoke to the Apex Insurance personnel office.

"Did I understand correctly?" she asked as he hung up the phone. "You've ..."

Christian Stiller nodded. "The Apex Insurance Company doesn't know anything about a person called Carol West," he said quietly. "Nor is there an employee missing who fits her description."

***

It was afternoon when Christian Stiller parked his car in the High Dive car park. He stepped through the wide door under the neon sign and looked around. 'Office' was written on a simple wooden door. He knocked and entered.

There were two desks in the room. One was empty. The other was occupied by a girl.

The first thing he noticed were her eyes. They were large, dark and serious. She had black hair that left her delicate ears exposed and a full mouth with lips that were naturally red.

"I'd like to speak to the manager if I may," he said. "My name's Stiller. Superintendent Stiller of Scotland Yard."

She nodded gravely. "Mr Merton's in the kitchen. Taking in a new delivery. He'll be back any minute. Would you like to take a seat until then?"

He pulled up a chair and pointed out of the window. "That's your swimming pool, isn't it?"

She stood up and opened the window. Her movements were graceful and easy. "Yes," she said softly. "The water's drained now. It has to be changed, of course."

She looked out at the green lawn and the blue-tiled basin that now lay empty and useless.

"Mr Merton found the body, didn't he?" asked Christian cautiously.

"Yes, he did." She spoke excellent English, but he thought he heard a foreign sound in it. "He dived into the water and found her. Right after that, I joined him. I was just going to see Mr Cooper. He's staying here." She raised a slender bare arm and pointed over to the edge of the forest. "In one of the bungalows."

Christian stood up and joined her. "Are there only bungalows here to stay in – or regular guest rooms as well?"

"Only bungalows." The faint reflection of a smile flashed across her face. "It's more modern that way. It's very popular. People are clamouring to stay here. You understand?"

He nodded. "I see. Who actually stays here?"

"You want a list of the guests? I'll have to ask you to wait until Mr Merton..."

"Don't worry," he interrupted her, "we can deal with the list later. I mean: What kind of people usually stay here?"

She tilted her head to the side, considering. "Most of them are business people who come to London by car," she said slowly. "Many are from Liverpool or Manchester. They spend the night here and are in the city in a few minutes the next morning."

"They must be quite interesting people, I expect?" he prompted her.

She pursed her mouth contemptuously. "They're just walking moneybags. They think they can buy everything."

Unwillingly, she looked down at her body, of which the light summer dress did not hide much.

"So those are your type of guests?" he deflected.

"Oh..." She looked up, and he thought he saw her blush slightly under the tanned skin. "Yes. But besides, there are guests coming from London too. People with money who are happy to get out of town for a weekend during the hot weather. Who don't want to go to the seaside because there's not enough time or because it's too crowded for them."

"And of course people who call themselves Mr and Mrs Smith or Brown or Jones," Christian stated matter-of-factly. "You don't have to look at me so startled, Miss..."

"Nagy, Julia Nagy. I'm Hungarian."

"You're a refugee?"

"Yes – since the Budapest uprising."

"Now, Miss Nagy, you needn't be alarmed. I've nothing to do with the vice squad. But you don't have to be a specialist to see that this is the ideal love nest for people who – well, let's say: don't want to be seen together in town."

She looked at him dismissively. "I'm not authorised to talk to you about our guests," she said coolly.

"Nor about Mr Cooper?" he asked.

"Oh, him!" A small smile softened the sternness of her face. "Our early riser. He's an old gentleman. Very kind – and more polite than most. But you can only talk to him about Babylon and Egypt."

"He's the scholarly type, eh?"

"A private scholar, I think he calls himself. He's not interested in anything that isn't at least five thousand years old."

"Then you are most certainly too young to be of interest to him?" asked Christian with a smile.

"Most definitely," she replied, smiling as well. "If I were an Egyptian mummy, he would love me. But like this ..."

"A real scholar, then. A bit like a scatty professor, would you say?"

"A bit, yes. He always leaves something lying around and then looks for it. But he's really nice. He really is. He reminds me of my ..."

She broke off.

"He reminds you of who?" Christian asked greedily.

"Oh – of a man I once knew," she evaded the question. She turned away from the window and went back to her desk.

Christian was about to sit down as well when the door opened. Victor Merton entered and twisted his mouth into a polite smile under his thin moustache.

"Superintendent Stiller, I presume?"

Christian bowed slightly.

"I'm Merton, the manager here. What can I do for you?"

"I'd like to take a look at the place where you found the dead woman, if you please, sir."

"The pool? Well, you can see it from here."

"I know. But I'm also interested in the area around it. If you'll be so kind..."

The phone rang and Julia Nagy picked up the receiver.

"Hello?" Then she handed the receiver to Christian. "It's for you, Mr Stiller."

He answered it. For seconds he heard only the sound of the line. Then a soft, polite voice said, "Is that Superintendent Stiller from Scotland Yard?"

"Yes, speaking."

"I want to warn you," the voice said. "Leave this case alone. You're in over your head. This business is too tough for you."

There was a crackling on the line. The caller had hung up. Christian handed the receiver back to the secretary. Then he turned to Merton. "Shall we go, sir?"

The manager ushered him out.

As they approached the pool Stiller asked Merton to explain to him exactly what had happened that morning.

"You see, I jumped off this board into the pool."

"Didn't you notice anything before doing so? Surely the water was clear?"

"It was quite transparent," Merton confirmed. "But if you jump into the water in the same place every day, you don't look at all. Besides, the sun was blinding me."

"Those are the bungalows over there, aren't they?" asked Christian, pointing to a row of small buildings.

"Yes, that's where our guests stay," the manager confirmed. "There aren't many. I can show you a list of the guests later."

"I'd like that, thank you very much. By the way, do your guests always drive on the lawn?"

"What? What do you mean?" Merton looked at him, puzzled.

"There's a clear wheel track leading to the swimming pool."

"That must have been the ambulance that took away the dead woman."

"Wait a minute – this is where you jumped into the water – this is where you found the girl. Where did you pull her out? Here?"

"No," Merton said, shaking his head. "On the other side, of course."

"Then the ambulance must have stopped over there, surely?"

"You're right. It was on the right. Not so close to the pool either. More like on the path."

"Has the lawn been mowed today?"

"No. But why...?"

"Thank you, that's enough for now. Now if we could go to your office?"

11

Christian didn't feel like talking to the man about his observations. He was sure that the tyre tracks were more than a few hours old, that they came from the previous night. That they belonged to the car that had brought Carol West here.

But he was also sure that Merton knew more than he was letting on.

The list of staff was unproductive. People had made their statements. He would find them on his desk. As would anything else that could be learned about the staff.

What about the guests?

"Two were only here for one night," Merton said. "They left early this morning. They were textile manufacturers who had to go to a conference. The police took down their names and addresses."

He looked at Christian questioningly.

"All right," he nodded, "and what about the others?"

"There's Mr Cooper, Mr George Cooper. He's about sixty years old. A regular guest of ours. He comes for a couple of weeks every year when the heat gets too much for him in town."

"Who else is there?" asked Christian.

"There's the Beckworths – Eve and John. They've been staying here for a week. They're from Blackpool. I've no idea what they're doing here. Do you, Miss Nagy?" he turned to the secretary standing silently by.

"I – I'm sorry, I don't know," she stammered, startled. Then she pulled herself together. "Mrs Beckworth said something about some relatives they were going to see. Besides, they usually go into town in the evening..."

Merton laughed. "She's a fun-loving lady, if you know what I mean," he said confidentially. "Much younger than her husband. I think she just drags him around so he can pay the bills afterwards."

"Were they here last night too?"

"I didn't see them yesterday. But they weren't here in the evening. Probably they didn't come back till very late."

"About what time would you say?"

Merton looked at Julia Nagy. She raised her slim shoulders.

"That's hard to say. The last guests who go into town rarely arrive back before two in the morning. There's always noise until then."

"But what about their keys?"

"The guests keep them as long as they are staying here," Merton said. "That way they are made to feel quite at home. Even the maid only enters the bungalows at the request of the guest."

Christian looked out of the window.

"Is that them?"

"Yes." Merton winked at him. "An unlikely pair, aren't they?"

"Hmm, they're not unusual," Christian defended himself. He watched the couple until they disappeared between the trees. He was a roundish man, whose hair was already thinning, and she a tall, slender woman with youthful movements.

"Last night," Julia Nagy said hesitantly, "last night I heard a car. It will have been Beckworth's."

"What time approximately?" asked Christian.

"Just before sunrise. It was just getting a little light. A very little."

"Can you see the swimming pool from your window?"

She shook her head. "No. It's just on the other side."

"Thank you, Miss Nagy. Mr Merton, was that all the guests you had staying last night?"

"That was everyone," the manager confirmed.

"Only four bungalows were let? That's not good for business, is it?"

"People are away on holiday," sighed the manager. "But it gets better at the weekend."

"Four out of ten bungalows," Christian reasoned. "There are ten, aren't there?"

Merton nodded in confirmation.

Christian looked at the map. "Number one has Mr Cooper and number three is Mr and Mrs Beckworth, that's right, isn't it?"

Again the manager nodded. The seemingly pointless questions seemed to make him nervous.

"Then why is the key to number ten missing from the board here?" Christian shot off his next question.

Merton didn't bat an eyelid. "The key? Oh yes, I see. You don't have to worry about that, Superintendent. Number ten is reserved for the boss."

"Who's that?"

"The owner of the High Dive. Mr Lombard."

"Do you mean Eddie Lombard?" asked Christian in surprise.

"Why, yes – do you know him?"

"I think so," Christian Stiller replied.

***

Sergeant Moore was waiting for him at the Yard. He was a stocky, middle-aged man, with red eyes – and the tenacity of the typical Englishman. He was Stiller's most reliable assistant. Even from the time when he was still an Inspector.

"The postmortem on Carol West won't be held until tomorrow, sir," he reported. "But I've no doubt that she was murdered."

"Neither do I," Christian said, sitting down at his desk. "By the way, do you know who owns High Dive? It's Eddie Lombard!"

"You mean Tomato Eddie?"

"That's the one."

"Damn," Moore said thoughtfully. "That's going to be a tough one to deal with."

Christian grinned.

"Someone else told me that today. But first, get a pot of coffee, will you?"

As they sipped the hot beverage, he went over the day's events with Moore. The staff review had revealed nothing new.

"We've combed the whole area, sir," Moore told him. "Did you know there's a school beyond the woods? The headmaster wasn't there. But a young teacher gave me some information. Long's his name. A skinny little fellow who looks like he doesn't get anything to eat. Anyway, he was terribly upset about what had happened at his neighbours. High Dive must be a real den of iniquity if you can believe him. Half-naked people, not married either, a bad example for his students and so on according to him. You know the type."

"He knew nothing else?"

"No facts. Just gossip and tittle-tattle. There may be some truth in it, of course. But what use is that to us?"

"Not much," Christian admitted. "Although jealousy is, after all, a motive for murder."

Moore waved his cup defensively.

"It can't be jealousy. Then the dead woman would have to have been known at the High Dive. But everyone's seen her photo, and everyone assured me that they'd never met her."

"And you don't think it's possible that someone could be lying?"

"Just the one person, you mean? There could be several. In a place like that, you're known to everyone – or you're known to no one at all."

"Several?" Christian pondered. "Why not several, actually? If Lombard has a hand in it?"

The phone rang. Christian picked it up.

He recognised the soft, polite voice immediately.

"Listen," said the stranger. "Have you considered properly my warning?"

"I beg your pardon? I can't hear you very well. Could you speak up a bit please!"

As he shouted into the mouthpiece, he hastily wrote on a piece of paper, "GET CALLER IDENTIFIED AND ARRESTED!"

Moore looked over his shoulder, nodded and ran out.

"Do you understand me better now?" the caller asked with emphatic enunciation.

"Yes, it's better now. What did you want to ask me?"

The other repeated his words.

"What's your interest in all this? Who are you anyway?"

It sounded as if the stranger laughed softly. "You don't seriously think I'm going to tell you that, do you?"

"But you're asking me to believe you. Even though I don't know you who you are!"

It didn't matter what he said. If he could just hold the man on the line for a few minutes.

"I see you won't be dissuaded," said the other. "Well, from now on, you watch yourself, especially when you go home at night."

"What d'you mean by that?"

"Exactly what I say. Look in all the dark corners, Superintendent. Someone might be waiting for you."

Moore came back in. He scribbled something on the note and slid it to Christian.

"BELHAMPTON. PUBLIC CALL BOX. PATROL CAR EN-ROUTE."

"Do you have any particular reasons for your nice warning?" asked Christian, just to say something.

"Many," came the reply. "But now I'm hanging up. Otherwise your patrol car will be here before I can disappear. Good night, Mr Stiller."

Christian put the phone down.

"Has he rung off?" the sergeant asked.

"Yes."

"Was it the same man who called you earlier on?"

Christian nodded. "He's a smart fellow. Said he was going to hang up before our patrol got there."

Moore whistled through his teeth. "He's a real sharp one. Knows his way around Scotland Yard, that's for sure. What did he want, anyway?"

"The same as before. To intimidate me. Tell me to watch out for muggings in the dark."

"H'm," the sergeant went on, "advice like that doesn't get any worse just because it comes from a crook, does it, sir?"

"What d'you mean...?"

"I'd really watch out if I were you, Chief."

***

These words came back to haunt Christian Stiller when he stopped in front of his house two hours later.

The street was dark. Much darker than usual. But there was always...

The lantern wasn't lit!

He got out of his car, slammed the door and locked it. Should he be afraid – just because an anonymous caller... Was there someone there? In the shade of the bushes – next to his front door? He hesitated. Should he unlock the door of his car again? He had a torch in there.

But that was ridiculous! He gave himself a shake and walked towards the house.

There was nothing to see. He only sensed the movement. He threw himself to the side. The sandbag only hit his shoulder. His left shoulder. He punched with his right. With a quick sidestep, he dodged the next attack.

A right hook – a hit! He felt the other one give way. He heard the other man groan. He pushed. Left – right! Then he curled up with a groan. He tried to grab the foot before he could kick it twice in the body. The other man fell on him and pushed him to the ground and searched for his throat with his hands.

He jerked one knee up and heard the grunt as the other ran out of air. He staggered up to his feet, still half defenceless. The other came up too and lunged at him. Punched and hit. His legs were like lead. He caught one blow with his shoulder and took the next one on the lowered skull.

Then he heard the snap of a flick-knife. The vicious roar brought him to his senses. As the shadowy opponent leapt at him, he let himself fall and threw himself around with all his might.

The other man fell like a tree with his knife clanking on the stones. Christian struggled to get up. His eyes flickered from the effort. But he had to find the weapon before the other ... Too late!

Panting, he leaned against the wall of the house. His arms half raised in defence.

A knife flashed at him.

CHAPTER TWO

Tomato Eddie

Christian Stiller saw the flash of the blade. In the faint glow of a distant streetlight, he couldn't clearly see his opponent's movements.

Christian had his aching arms half raised in defence. His legs were like lead.

Then came the attack. He made a quick leap to the side.

That was his luck.

There was a clang as the hand with the knife hit the wall. At that moment, Christian grabbed it, gripped the wrist and he let himself fall and spun around.

The other man fell over him. He hit the stones hard. He lay there for a moment. Then he jumped up, standing on unsteady legs. He looked around for Christian.

Then Christian found him and landed a right, and a left. Then another right.

There wasn't the right amount of force behind them. Christian knew it. But the punches were enough for his opponent. The man in front of him only grunted and he turned away. Christian's next blow hit his back. Involuntarily, the detective stopped his attack. To hit an opponent in the back – that wasn't right. That wasn't fair. The other took advantage of the pause. Staggering, he began to run. Then with faster and faster steps.

There was no point in running after him. Christian thought of his car. Where the hell were his keys?

He felt around in his pockets. Nothing. Were they lost? He found his lighter and shone the light on the ground. He found the car keys after two minutes of searching. He ran to the car and unlocked it with hands still trembling with exertion.

But by the time he started the engine and drove down the road with his headlights on, there was no sign of his assailant. Disgruntled, he turned around and drove back to his house. He parked the car, unlocked the front door and slowly climbed the few steps to the lift. All his limbs ached.

When he got to his flat he found there was an envelope in the letterbox. It was addressed to him in block letters and without a return address.

Automatically, he tore open the envelope while turning on the light in his study.

The telephone rang. He threw the envelope on the desk and picked up the receiver. "Kensington 9856," he said.

"Ah, there you are," said a soft, polite voice.

"Yes, here I am," he replied mockingly. "I suppose that surprises you?"

"Not at all," the other replied in the same tone. "On the contrary, I'm glad you've come home in one piece. You are in one piece, I hope?"

Without saying a word, Christian hung up the phone.

The man was well informed. Or was he? If he was the person who had hired the knife hero – and Christian had no doubt that he was – then perhaps he just wanted to make sure that his man had been successful.

Christian went into the bathroom and looked at himself in the mirror.

He wasn't a pretty sight. There were abrasions on his forehead. There was a large, bloodied spot under his left eye, which was already starting to swell and his mouth was also slightly swollen. He reached for the iodine bottle.

When he returned to the study, he saw the opened letter lying there. He reached for it and pulled out a piece of paper. It was blank. There was only a hastily done drawing on it. It showed the face of a pretty young girl.

It was the face of Carol West!

He held the paper carefully by the edge. He could have bet that no one would have been stupid enough to leave fingerprints on it. But it would have been against his nature to miss even the slightest possibility.

It was ordinary paper. And an envelope of the kind you could probably buy in any stationery shop in London. He couldn't expect any clue from this.

But who could've sent him this drawing – and why? To confuse him? To draw his attention in the wrong direction?

Then maybe it wasn't about Carol West at all? Wasn't the girl's murder the main thing? Was it really about something else? Something more serious than murder? Or was that the impression the killer was trying to give him? His head was throbbing. No, there was no point. He wouldn't solve the mystery tonight, he decided.

***

"And yet Carol West is the key figure!" he said aloud as he stood under the shower the next morning.

The dead woman was his only clue. And not a bad one. The attack proved he was on the right track. Not on the trail of a single man, but of a gang. For his brawny attacker from the previous evening was certainly not the same man who asked him such impertinent questions on the phone in such a cultivated voice.

After breakfast he phoned the Yard. Sergeant Moore had no news for him. He was astonished when his boss told him in brief about the attack the previous evening.

"You must be more careful, sir. I did warn you," he urged. "If it had been two..."

"If!" Christian raised his shoulders, oblivious to the fact that the sergeant couldn't see the gesture. "You want me to wrap myself in cotton wool and let six men guard me? That's our occupational hazard, and you know it."

"Then at least tell me where you're going all the time," Moore begged.

"So you can guard me?"

"No, so we don't have to start all over again if – if something happens to you."

Christian couldn't object to that argument. "Okay," he said. "I'm going to Eddie Lombard's now."

"Have you made an appointment?"

"No. Maybe I can surprise him before he's got time to make up any excuses."

He hung up and left the flat. Slowly he descended the stairs.

Then he stood in the street. Involuntarily, he looked around in all directions. It was the usual sight. There were a few parked cars, housewives on their way to the shops and children playing.

Christian went to his car. He was about to unlock the door when a bright voice behind him said, "I wouldn't do that, sir!" Christian looked around. There was a little boy standing there. Maybe he was about eight years old. He had a cowboy hat on his head and a wide gun-belt around his hips with two dangerous-looking bang-bang colts.

"Well, why not, my boy?" the detective asked with a smile. The little boy looked up at him seriously, obviously convinced of his importance. "There was someone at your car, sir!"

Christian listened. Nothing was unimportant after last night. "When?" he asked.

"Early this morning, before it got really light," the little boy said seriously.

"What did he look like?"

"I don't know," came the reply. "It was still too dark for me so see that."

"How is it that you saw him at all?" continued Christian. "You weren't out on the street at that time, were you?"

"Of course not," the boy replied, pushing his hat back onto his neck with the casual hand gesture he had watched Roy Rogers do on television. "I couldn't sleep, but I mustn't wake my parents too early. So I looked out of the window. We live next door here."

"And that's when you saw someone come and tamper with my car?"

"He even crawled under it."

"What did you do then?"

"I looked out of the window until it was light enough for me to come out on to the street. I had to warn you, Mr Stiller!"

"You know me?"

"Sure," the boy replied, beaming. "We're neighbours, aren't we? What are you going to do now?"

Christian fished a coin out of his pocket and handed it to him. "This is for you. I'm going to see if you're a good boy first."

The little boy held the money in his open hand. He looked at Christian doubtfully. That wasn't why he'd been paying attention here after all. Not for money!

"Go ahead and take it," Christian said. "Good deeds are rewarded. That's the way it should be. And now you have to promise me something: Go to your mother and don't come near this car again until the police have been here, do you hear me?"

"But I..." the boy stammered.

"You want to know what happens next, is that it?" asked Christian. His little friend nodded vigorously.

"Fine. I'll come and find you in a few days when it's all over. Then I'll tell you how it went. And thanks again!"

When the little boy was gone, Christian Stiller walked carefully around his car. There was nothing to see from the outside. The windows and doors were closed. Nor did he see anything conspicuous inside the car.

Then he remembered that Johnny had said the man had even crawled under the car. He bent down and looked.

He didn't hear a car brake close behind him.

"Can we help, sir?" a voice asked.

He didn't know afterwards how he had got up so quickly with his muscle tear.

It was a patrol car. The officer next to the driver had his head stuck out of the window.

"How did you get here, Johnson?" asked Christian.

"Oh, we just happened to be in the area, sir," the man evaded.

Christian realised that Sergeant Moore had begun to hold his protective hand over him. There was no point in getting angry about unsolicited help now. On the contrary, the patrol was very welcome to him.

"Come over here with your torch," he said. The uniformed man got out.

"Shine it under my car and tell me if you see anything unusual," Christian ordered.

Johnson went into a push-up position and looked under the vehicle. After a while he straightened up.

"There's a black wire, sir," he reported. "On the underneath, it's taped down. On the top it leads to the bodywork. If you want me to give my opinion ..."

"Yes?"

"We had something like that in a course I went on. I wouldn't be surprised if there wasn't a detonator at the top of it. And a whole lot of explosives. Lucky you saw that in time, sir!"

"I didn't see anything," Christian said. "A young lad who lives next door pointed it out to me. We'll have to make him an honorary member of Scotland Yard, if there is such a thing. Right – you've got a radio in the car, haven't you? Call the Yard. Get an explosives expert here immediately. You'd better close off the road as well."

***

Christian took a taxi to Eddie Lombard's after this incident. His office was in a run-down East End building. A busty blonde let him in and led him to the boss's outer office, where an even better rounded and even brighter bleached young lady sat.

"You want to see the boss?" she asked.

Christian nodded. "Yes. On an extremely urgent matter!" he said.

She hesitated. "May I have your name ..."

"Stiller. Christian Stiller."

"From which company shall I say?"

"Just say the name. That'll do."

It was obviously enough. Besides, there had to be a microphone here, anyway. The door to the boss's room opened and Eddie Lombard hurried in. He was a lean, thick-skinned man in his mid-forties. Surprised, almost frightened, the secretary looked at him. But Eddie paid no attention to her.

"Ah, what a rare visitor do we have here!" he exclaimed with mock surprise. "Do you want to see me, Superintendent? Who else might you want to see? Well, Nellie here, for instance. You have no idea how many visitors I've had since Nellie started working for me."

Nellie tried to put on an innocent face.

"Come on, Superintendent," Lombard said with an inviting wave of his hand, "come through to my office."

Christian entered the office of the man who had roamed London with a fruit cart twenty-five years ago and whom they now called the secret king of London nightlife. At any rate Lombard, who had retained the nickname Tomato Eddie from his youth, owned more nightclubs and restaurants than anyone else in the city. That he hadn't come by the money honestly could be counted on the fingers of every little policeman. He had also been in court a few times for all kinds of offences. But in the end, the judges always let him off because there was nothing to prove.

"Please sit down, Superintendent," Eddie said, smiling. "What can I offer you? A cigar? A cigarette? Whisky? Gin? Nothing? That's a pity."

He sat down behind his desk, which was as ostentatious as the whole room with its heavily upholstered furniture and the thick plush carpet, in which Christian discovered the elongated burn marks of cigarettes. Apparently it wasn't always fine people Eddie dealt with. "I can guess what you came for," Eddie's deep voice droned on. Christian looked at him politely. He still didn't speak.

"You've come about Carol West!" said Lombard, looking at him dismissively.

"That's right," Christian replied. "You own the High Dive, don't you?"

"Of course it's mine," Lombard affirmed. "Am I supposed to deny it just because someone was killed there?"

"What kind of man is the manager of High Dive?" he asked.

"Who – Merton? His colleagues call him the handsome Victor." Lombard grinned. "He's a capable fellow. He's good at what he does and he's got plenty of experience. His accounts are right, too. I can't say anything bad about him. Maybe he's a bit crazy. He's a sporting type. Especially when there's girls around. But everyone has a little weakness, don't they, Superintendent? Better him running around in his trunks than stealing wallets. At least he'll attract a few more guests. Old boys and the like. They can't be stopped when they see Victor. And the young ones aren't much better."

Christian thought of Julia Nagy. She didn't seem particularly impressed with Merton. But perhaps he had been mistaken....

"...wanted to say," he heard Lombard continue. "The things that have happened in my clubs – you have no idea. Yesterday we caught a guy at the White Horse with a pair of scissors in his pocket. He used them to cut the girls' clothes off in the back."

"What did you do to him?" asked Christian, just to say something.

"We politely asked him to repair the damage," Eddie said in the tone of a man of honour. "The boy is loaded. By the way, that reminds me ..."

Christian took it upon himself to bring the case to the attention of the blackmail squad.

"I need to wet my whistle," Eddie said, pouring gin into a water glass.

Christian realised that he would never get anywhere if he let the man prattle on.

"Are you sure Carol West was murdered at High Dive?" he asked.

Lombard choked on the gin and took a while to catch his breath. "Where else would she have been murdered?" he finally managed to say.

Christian made an indifferent face. "I don't know. That's why I'm asking you."

Lombard grinned. It looked a little laboured. "Oh, and Uncle Eddie is supposed to help his friends from the Yard, is he? Now that's quite a novel idea."

Christian raised his shoulders impassively. "After all, the body was found on your premises. You must have every interest in the case being solved as quickly as possible, if only so that no suspicion falls on you."

He watched the change in Lombard's countenance with interest. All artificial amusement disappeared from it. In its place was an expression of such malice that the detective no longer wondered at the respect Lombard enjoyed in the underworld. "You can count on it," Lombard groaned out. "If I catch the man that did it..." He mastered himself with a tremendous effort. For a moment he was silent. Then he said in his old, deliberately funny tone: "Then I'll take him to Scotland Yard myself, so he can get the punishment he deserves."

"Can you tell me anything about the staff at the High Dive?" asked Christian.

Lombard put the glass down and gave the detective a sly look. "You want me to tell you about little Julia, eh? She's a cute little doll, but as cold as a dog's snout. She pretends she doesn't even know men exist."

"I have no intention of testing Miss Nagy's temper," Christian said coolly. "I'm only interested in her because she works at High Dive. She's a refugee, isn't she?"

"Yes, from the East somewhere," Lombard replied indeterminately. "I don't care about that sort of thing. Not as long as people are doing their jobs."

"And they do?"

"Mostly," Lombard assured him. "There have been a few things, my goodness, after all, she needn't always be so snooty to the guests ..."

"To the male guests, you mean?" interposed Christian.

"Sure, sure. After all, a girl like that doesn't forgive herself anything if she's nice to a rich man. In any case, she doesn't need to slap anyone. I don't do that. I value a decent tone..."

"That's what you're known for," Christian said mockingly.

"Aren't I?" Eddie nodded. He didn't seem to notice the irony. "But otherwise I have nothing against little Nagy. After all, she's doing quite well as an embellishment to the place."

The man obviously had a mind like a hound dog. A guy like a bull, yet cunning and unburdened by any conscience.

"I keep order in my businesses," Eddie explained, "no ambiguous characters, no criminals, no addicts – all decent people. I always say that's the way it should be ..."

The door burst open. In the frame stood a broad-shouldered man with his hairline a finger's breadth above his eyebrows.

"Boss, the stupid goat doesn't want me..." He broke off and stared at the detective. His puffy mouth opened to reveal the gap where two incisors were missing. His right eye was almost closed and the left one was also bloodshot.

Involuntarily, Christian rubbed the cracked knuckles of his right hand. Then he turned to Lombard.

"What did you just say?" he stated dryly. "No one with a criminal record works for you?" He pointed to the man in the doorway. "Denny Winters is obviously a dark horse, then?"

Winters lowered his head and stared at him. Christian slid off his chair.

There was a bang from behind him. Sharp and dry. He heard the bullet whistle past his ear.

CHAPTER THREE

The Man Who Complained

Christian Stiller threw himself to the side. But before he could try to reach the door with a long leap, he was jerked around.

The shot hadn't been meant for him. Eddie Lombard sat calmly behind his desk – and put the pistol back in a drawer.

Denny Winters stared into space with glassy eyes, his hands pressed to his heart. Then he spun around long and hard and hit the floor. A cloud of dust rose from the carpet, on which a dark spot spread immediately afterwards.

Christian didn't need a second to adjust to the changed situation.

"Why did you shoot him?" he asked sharply.

Lombard looked at him coolly. "Because he wanted to murder you."

Christian didn't believe him. He was sure that Lombard had only got rid of an annoying confidant. He was also sure that Denny Winters was the man who had assaulted him the night before, and on Lombard's behalf. "Thank you for saving my life," he said mockingly. "But how will you explain that to the court? Self-defence – against a man with bare hands?"

Lombard didn't bat an eyelid. "First of all, I didn't want to shoot him. I wanted to hit his arm. That the shot went through his heart – that was bad luck. Secondly, you obviously didn't notice Winters reaching under his jacket when he came at you. That's why I fired."

Christian looked at him suspiciously.

If Winters was armed, then it would be difficult to prove Lombard guilty. He bent down and flipped back the dead man's jacket. Lombard was right. Denny Winters was carrying a knife under his left armpit. It had slipped halfway out of the leather sheath. No one would be able to prove whether Winters had pulled it out or whether it had slipped out due to the fall.

Christian Stiller straightened up. Only now did he see Lombard's secretary standing in the doorway. Her eyes widened in shock. Christian turned to Lombard. "I assume you have a licence for the gun?" he asked.

"Of course I do," Lombard replied. The tone of self-righteous respectability didn't match the brutality of his face.

"But once again they won't be able to prove anything against him," thought Christian.

"Good," he said, "then you'll allow me to use your telephone. In the meantime, don't touch anything."

***

Silence reigned in the gloomy corridors of Scotland Yard. It was midday. Christian hardly met a soul as he walked with long strides towards his office.

The interlude with Eddie Lombard had taken him two hours. That was two hours of wasted time. Nothing could be got out of Lombard. Nor would the judicial investigation of the incident reveal anything new. And Winters, the man he needed to talk to, was dead....

Sergeant Moore was waiting for him in the office. Christian briefed him with curt words. "What annoys me most is that I'll end up having to testify for him before the examining magistrate," he concluded.

Moore nodded. "I told you so, boss. By the way, there was a plastic bomb under your car."

Christian raised his shoulders. "I suspected as much. But what about Carol West? Any update on her? Wasn't the post-mortem supposed to be today?"

"It was, sir. As we assumed: Murder. She was strangled and then thrown into the water."

"How long after the murder?"

"Probably very soon after."

"What do you mean, probably?"

"That's what I asked Dr Hendricks. He says it's something to do with the connective tissue. Gave me a long lecture on..."

"Please don't repeat it," Christian interrupted him. "I'm not a medical doctor. What conclusion did the doctor come to?"

"He says he can only put on record that Miss West was strangled. By hand, and from the front. The larynx was crushed in the way only thumbs can do. In addition, the doctor concludes from various signs that it took less than a quarter of an hour for the body to be thrown into the water. He emphasises, however, that this is his private opinion. The signs are not so clear that they could be considered as evidence in court."

"At least it's a clue." Christian pondered. "Did the dead woman have any other injuries?"

"None, sir. That's just it. If you ask me, I'd say she knew her killer."

"Knew her killer and thought he was harmless, you mean?"

"Exactly, sir. Otherwise she wouldn't have let him get so close. She would've fought back. Then the doctor would've found traces of a struggle."

Christian stood up and began to walk around the room.

"The thought is obvious, of course," he said finally. "But there's something wrong with it. Judging by the execution, it would be an ordinary murder. If you only look at the crime itself, you would have to say: Carol West met secretly with a lover, and in a fit of jealousy he strangled her. Then he threw her in the pool, thinking we couldn't tell she hadn't drowned."

"So not a career criminal, you think?" Moore added.

"Right." Christian stopped at the window and looked out. "A murder committed by someone living somewhere near the

High Dive. Let's say fifteen minutes from there at the most, if we're to believe Dr Hendricks."

He turned and looked at Moore. "But what's Eddie Lombard got to do with it? Surely the old fox wouldn't have wilfully aroused suspicion by having the girl murdered and thrown into the swimming pool of his own hotel?"

"Certainly not," confirmed the sergeant.

"But if he had nothing to do with the murder," Christian continued, "why did he interfere? Why did he send Denny Winters after me last night? He claims he employed Winters as some kind of errand boy. He claims not to have known about Denny's criminal record. That's a blatant lie, by the way."

"Indeed it is," Moore said. "It must have been an embarrassing surprise for him that Winters came storming into his office at the very moment you were there. Clearly, he shot him on purpose. But we can't prove that."

"I want to know what he has to do with our case. If he didn't order the murder, why is he trying to intimidate me or even get rid of me? There can only be one explanation."

"Namely that you're becoming dangerous to him," the sergeant added. "Maybe he's running an illegal side business out at High Dive. Narcotics perhaps ..."

"No way," Christian objected. "Narcotics is what he would be dealing with in town. In nightclubs where lots of people get together. Where no one knows anyone else. But out at the High Dive? He could be standing in Trafalgar Square with the stuff."

"But then what's he got to hide out there?" asked Moore. "If the High Dive really is a den of iniquity, as Robin Long says..."

"That's the young teacher you spoke to, is it?"

"Yes, sir. He's a strange man. But suppose he's right and there really are such immoral goings-on at High Dive.

Suppose you were to find out about it. That wouldn't be so bad for Eddie that he'd have to have a Scotland Yard Superintendent killed because of it, surely."

Involuntarily, Christian had to smile at the indignation that resonated in those words. "Thank you very much for your confidence, Sergeant. But you're right. So far we've no motive for Lombard's behaviour. Besides, we don't know who the man with the polite voice was who called me yesterday."

"One of Lombard's men, possibly?"

"I don't think so. Why should he have me threatened if his man is already sitting in the bushes waiting for me? And then, who put the bomb under my car? Was that one of Lombard's men, too?" He went to the door. "Come on, Moore. We'll go to High Dive and have another go at the people there. My car's downstairs, isn't it?"

"Yes, the explosives guys are done with it. By the way, what's the name of the school where this Mr Long teaches?"

***

When they had passed the cottages on the edge of Belhampton, Christian asked, "Does the road to St. Christopher's Boarding School turn off before or after High Dive?"

"Before," said Moore. "But you said you didn't you want to..."

"I've thought it over," Christian replied. "We'll question the philanthropic Mr Long again first."

After a bend in the road, the boarding school was suddenly in front of them. In the middle was a typical English country house. Around it was a row of single-storey buildings: the students' classrooms and dormitories.

They drove over the crunching gravel of the driveway and stopped in front of the portal. A man in overalls, he might be a caretaker or a gardener, showed them the way to the office.

An elderly, friendly and somewhat worldly-looking gentleman rose as they entered. "My name is Corbett and I'm the headmaster of this school. Is there something I can do for you, Mister...?"

"Stiller," Christian said. "This is Mr Moore here. We'd like to speak to your Mr Long on a private matter. I hope he's not teaching in class at the moment?"

The headmaster cradled his head thoughtfully. "No, he doesn't have lessons right now, but you will hardly be able to speak to him anyway. Mr Long wasn't feeling well this morning. He's in his room."

Christian nodded sympathetically. "Being a teacher's not an easy job, I suppose?"

The headmaster smiled. "It's not so hard if you love the profession."

"And Mr Long doesn't love it?" asked Christian.

"I dare not decide that," replied the headmaster cautiously. "But you see, he is young. Since he bought the car..." He sighed a little helplessly.

"You mean he's out a lot in the evenings?" asked Christian. He was a little ashamed that he had led the good man around by the nose like that. But it didn't help.

The headmaster took off his glasses and began to clean them. "He has a right to his evenings out," he said. "The times have changed. Even we old schoolmen have to adapt. A young man is entitled to his free time, even if he is a teacher." He put his glasses back on and looked at Christian with a mischievous smile. "Though I must admit it used to be easier to work – with teachers who came to class fresh in the morning because they went to bed early the previous evening, instead of driving around in a car."

"Would you mind if we tried to see if Mr Long would see us anyway?" asked Christian.

"Not at all," said the headmaster obligingly. "I'll show you the way."

They climbed a flight of stairs. The wooden steps were old and they creaked loudly. Somewhere a school class was reciting a poem. Sergeant Moore sniffed. "It smells like gas in here," he said.

The smell got stronger the higher they went. At the top of the corridor, the headmaster stopped. "Indeed." He drew in an audible breath. "Now I smell it too."

Moore pushed him aside. He pointed to the left. "That's where it's coming from."

"What's here? Is it the kitchen?" asked Christian hastily.

The headmaster shook his head helplessly. "No. Only Mr Long lives on the left."

The sergeant was already at the door of the room, Christian two steps beside him. He pressed down the handle but the door didn't give.

"Break it open," said a choked voice behind him. He looked around. The headmaster held the handkerchief pressed in front of his mouth.

Christian took a running start and kicked the door with his foot. Wood splintered. It was brittle, old wood. The door was open, but only a crack.

It didn't give any further. There was a resistance from the inside.

"Come on!" gasped Christian. Moore braced himself against the door beside him. A jerk – then something moved inside. It was a cupboard. There was an almighty crash as it toppled.

They almost fell into the room. A hiss pulled them up. With a leap, Christian stood at the cooker and turned off the gas. The sergeant ran to the window and pushed the sashes wide open.

Then they grabbed the man who was lying motionless on the bed. Coughing and gasping for breath, they carried him out. They stumbled down the stairs and laid him on the grass outside.

Automatically, Moore began artificial respiration while Christian ran to the phone.

***

The ambulance pulled up beside them. "It was gas," Christian said to the doctor jumping out. "Clearly a suicide attempt. And when you're done: inside in the office is the headmaster. I think it's a heart attack."

The doctor nodded and bent over the teacher. While he was listening to his heart with the stethoscope, a second car arrived. It pulled up sharply.

"Is that him?" asked Sergeant Ingram from the Belhampton police station as he got out. Then he recognised Christian. "Oh, good afternoon, sir, I'm sorry, I didn't recognise you right away."

"This is Mr Long," said Christian. "A teacher at this school. It was a suicide attempt."

"Robin Long?" the uniformed man asked. "You mean the crazy one?"

"Why do you call him crazy? What do you know ...?" He interrupted himself. The doctor had straightened up. "He's still alive," he said. "He must go to hospital immediately. Help the driver get him into the ambulance, please. Where's the office?"

Christian led him to the old man. The headmaster was lying in an armchair, gasping for breath. Several men stood around him, perplexed.

"Sit down," the doctor said. He put his bag on the table, opened it and began to fill a syringe.

Christian went out. The two sergeants were just about to lift Long into the ambulance, then it pulled away.

"Why do you think Robin Long's crazy?" Christian wanted to know from Sergeant Ingram.

"Because he keeps pestering us with complaints," the officer said grimly. "He's filed four complaints against the High Dive management alone for endangering public morals."

"Of what kind?" asked Christian.

"The usual, sir. The couples who stay there are not supposed to be married to each other. Besides, they are supposed – in Mr Long's opinion – to do all sorts of things in public."

"And is there any truth in all that?" asked Christian.

"Nothing," said Sergeant Ingram crossly. "The first time we fell for it and we went to see the High Dive. We were meant to find supposedly naked people cavorting about the place. But they were swimming in the swimming pool and had normal swimming costumes and trunks on."

"And the unmarried couples?"

"Nothing to prove, sir, certainly no fault of the manager."

"So there was no reason to intervene?"

"No, sir. Long is one of those lunatics who smell immorality everywhere because there's something wrong with themselves."

"Thank you, Sergeant. Come on, Moore, let's have another look at his room."

Sergeant Ingram saluted and got into his car. Christian went into the house with Moore. As they climbed the stairs, Moore said: "A man like Long, couldn't he commit a murder, do you think? A murder like the one of Carol West?"

"Certainly he could," Christian confirmed. "But unfortunately, as far as we know, he hasn't any connections with Eddie Lombard. Come in, let's have a look around."

The room still smelled of gas. Nothing else was out of the ordinary.

They put the cupboard back in its place. "He moved it in front of the door himself," Moore said. "And the cracks in the window were taped with paper." He looked around. "The room doesn't have a second entrance either. So it really was a suicide attempt, sir."

Christian rummaged in the desk drawer. "Indeed," he replied. "In the meantime, take a look in the cupboard, Moore."

The sergeant set to work. There were only a few articles of clothing. He picked up a coat and reached into the pockets. A half-crumbled cigarette was the only haul.

He reached for a jacket. Then he whistled through his teeth. Christian turned around. "Do you have something there?"

"Here – this note!" Moore held out a piece of paper to him. "There's a number written on it," he said hoarsely.

"Is it Kensington 9856?" asked Christian.

"That's right, chief. But how did you know ...?"

"It's clearly written all over your puzzled face," Christian said dryly. "Besides, half of England seems to be interested in my phone number at the moment."

He looked out of the window. "By the way, we're being watched. No, stay away from the window. We don't have to give ourselves away."

"Can you recognise anyone, sir?"

"Not really. At first I just saw two dots flashing in the sun. Over by the edge of the forest."

"Someone with binoculars, you think?"

"Definitely. But the air is so hazy from the heat that I can't make out much. There's a bright spot, half hidden behind a tree. That's all. At least the forest is a few hundred yards away. Are you done, by the way? Good. Then we'll say goodbye to the headmaster and be on our way."

"And what about the observer? What are we going to do about them?"

"It's very simple," Christian said and descended the creaking stairs. "We'll be waiting."

"Do you know where they'll come out of the forest?" the sergeant asked in wonder.

"I think so."

"And where's that?"

"Where all our tracks converge," Christian Stiller said. "At the High Dive."

CHAPTER FOUR

An Odd Couple

There were about two dozen cars in the High Dive car park. "Murder seems to be good for business," Christian Stiller remarked dryly. Then he turned the corner and headed for the terrace. Sergeant Moore followed him. They found a free table, adjusted the colourful parasol and sat down.

"They really seem to be enjoying it," Moore said, glancing at the freshly filled swimming pool and the sunbathing lawn. Both were well occupied. The terrace was also a colourful, peaceful scene. There was nothing to indicate that the majority of the guests had only come because they had read about Carol West's murder in their newspapers.

"We don't want to be uncharitable," Christian replied. "Curiosity is only human. Now we have to be careful. I've chosen this spot so that we can watch the edge of the forest behind the bungalows. So – we just sit here and wait."

They ordered tea. When they were alone again, the sergeant asked: "Chief, why are you so sure that the person who was watching us will come out of the forest at this very spot?"

Christian smiled without taking his eyes off the edge of the forest. "Because the High Dive is the centre of this whole case."

"You mean: because Carol West's body was found here and because Robin Long tried to kill himself not far from here?"

"Not to mention Eddie Lombard," Christian said. "He owns the High Dive. He set Denny Winters on me, don't forget."

"And shot him before Denny could say anything," Moore added.

"There's also the man with the soft, polite voice," Christian reminded him.

"Right! He called you from Belhampton! At least the one time we were able to trace the call."

"And the first time he called me here at the High Dive office," Christian added, "I'd only just arrived a few minutes previously. So he must have been around here somewhere."

"Couldn't it have been Lombard?"

"No. Tomato Eddie's not an actor. That wasn't his voice."

"Or the teacher?"

"Long? I don't think so. In the first place, he couldn't leave the boarding school during the day, and in the second place – why should he want to arouse suspicion?"

The sergeant shook his head. "He's made himself suspicious by the suicide attempt anyway, and – sir, there's someone coming towards us."

Christian watched the man from the corner of his eye. He was short, roundish and maybe fifty years old.

"That's Beckworth," Moore said without moving his mouth. "John Beckworth. Businessman from Liverpool."

Mr Beckworth looked around searchingly. Then he came to their table. He was wearing a dark suit that would have suited the City rather than here. "It's a wonder he doesn't have a bowler hat on," Christian thought.

"You don't mind, do you?" asked Beckworth politely.

"But of course!" Christian made a hand gesture towards the two vacant chairs.

Beckworth wavered for a moment as to which one to take. Then he sat down, carefully smoothing out the creases.

The waiter came and brought the tea. Mr Beckworth ordered coffee and cake with whipped cream. "The cake here is excellent," he said with an apologetic smile. "I can highly recommend it."

Christian gave him a friendly nod.

Then he watched the edge of the forest again from half-closed eyes.

"Excuse me," the fat man turned to the sergeant, "haven't we met before?"

Christian nodded imperceptibly. Moore understood and took over the task of distracting Beckworth.

"I had the pleasure of meeting you yesterday, sir" he said.

"Oh yes – now I remember. You were the gentleman in plain clothes who asked us all if we knew the – I mean, if we knew the poor girl who was found here." He muffled his voice. "You're from Scotland Yard, aren't you?"

Moore nodded.

"Did you get anything out of all your questioning?" asked John Beckworth further. "There was just something in the paper about an unidentified dead woman."

"We know who she was now," Moore replied vaguely.

Beckworth leaned forward with interest. "Do you know who did it yet, too?"

Christian held his breath, but the sergeant was on guard.

"What makes you think it was murder?" he asked coolly back.

"Me? I – well, how else could she – I mean, she's not going to have jumped into the swimming pool fully clothed by herself," Beckworth stammered.

Moore shrugged his shoulders. "It may well have been an accident."

"But all these people here! If they thought it was an accident, they wouldn't all have come out here from London."

Christian bit back a smile as he heard Moore cornered with the same arguments he'd used himself earlier. But the sergeant was equal to the situation.

"Oh, you know what people are like!" It sounded convincingly haughty. "They always think of murder and manslaughter right away. In reality, they're mostly ordinary accidents."

"Ah, well I suppose you know what you're talking about," said Beckworth disappointedly. "Then you're not here on official business at all?"

"Not at all," lied the sergeant. "I had some business nearby and just wanted to have a quick cup of tea."

Christian paid no attention to the next words. He looked tensely over to the edge of the forest, where a bright spot had just appeared between the trees.

A clang startled him. Hot liquid burned on his ankle.

"I beg your pardon!" Beckworth made helpless gestures. "My cup – it suddenly dropped out of my hand." He pulled a large white cloth from his pocket and began to dab Christian's trousers.

"It's okay, accidents can happen." Christian took his leg from the helpless man. Then he looked towards the edge of the forest again.

But it was too late. The bright spot had disappeared. He thought he could still see the door of a bungalow being closed. Number three, he remembered. John and Eve Beckworth's. The mismatched couple, one half of whom had just distracted him so neatly.

So he didn't see Eve Beckworth disappearing into her bungalow? That she had binoculars with her?

Beckworth interrupted his thoughts. "Please excuse me again," he asked. "I can't think how it could have happened …"

The waiter came and swept up the broken pieces of the cup. "A new cup, please," Beckworth said. He touched Christian's hand with fleshy, warm, moist fingers. "I may, of course, reimburse you for the cost of cleaning?"

Christian gave up watching the bungalow. There was no point in making the purpose of his being here too obvious.

"Forget it, please," he said. "Don't let it spoil a nice day's holiday."

"Well, that's very kind of you …"

"You are here on holiday, I suppose?"

"Holiday?" Beckworth sighed. "You can't really call it a holiday. It's a family thing that's keeping us here."

"You're not here alone?" asked Christian with feigned innocence.

"No, my wife..." Beckworth made a half-hearted hand motion towards the lawn. "She's there somewhere. But – actually – here she comes!"

Christian looked over. From the pool came a woman. Blonde, tanned, tall and slim. Certainly twenty years younger than her husband. Christian recognised her despite the sunglasses she wore: this was Eve Beckworth.

They stood up as she approached the table.

"I saw you come over earlier, John." She tugged at the jacket of her short beach suit. Then she looked at Moore. "You were here yesterday, weren't you?"

Moore bowed affirmatively. Beckworth looked at Christian questioningly. "I beg your pardon. I'm afraid I can't introduce you. I don't know your name."

"Stiller," Christian said, watching Eve Beckworth's face carefully. "Christian Stiller." Had her eyes widened in shock? He couldn't see clearly through the dark lenses of her glasses.

"I'm Eve Beckworth," she said coolly. "Let's sit down."

The way John Beckworth moved the vacant chair to her seemed almost submissive.

"You look so serious," he said as they sat.

She seemed to force herself into a fleeting smile. "It's the heat," she said in an indifferent voice. "I've been lying in the sun too long, I think."

"You should have worn a hat," her husband said reproachfully.

She massaged the back of her neck as if to drive away a pain. "It'll be all right in a minute," she said.

The waiter stopped at their table. "No," Eve Beckworth said. "I don't want anything now. I think I'll rest a little. You'll excuse me, please." She stood up unsteadily. Her husband jumped up and took her arm. "I'll take you to the bungalow, my dear. Goodbye, gentlemen!"

Silently, Christian and the sergeant looked after the two.

"An odd couple, aren't they?" said a soft voice behind them.

Christian turned around. His eyes fell on the rubber soles of Victor Merton's shoes. They didn't quite match the elegant summer suit the manager of the High Dive was wearing.

Merton noticed the look. "You didn't hear me approach, did you? I hope I didn't startle you?"

"I'm not that easily startled," Christian defended. "Would you like to join us?"

"I think we'd better go to the office," Merton said. "It's excruciatingly hot out here." He ran a neatly folded handkerchief over his forehead. "I saw you sitting here through the window," he continued. "Just didn't want to disturb you while you were – ahem, not alone."

Christian stood up. "All right, let's go. I just have to pay quickly."

"Not at all," Merton defended himself. "You are, of course, my guests."

Followed by Sergeant Moore, they went inside. It was indeed pleasantly cool there.

"There's nothing like a good air-conditioning system," said Merton. "If I could only get Miss Nagy to keep the window closed, we'd have the most comfortable temperature."

Christian thought of the dark-haired girl with the large, serious eyes. "She'll be used to the warmth from Hungary," he said.

Merton looked at him in surprise. As if he wanted to ask a question. But then he just said, "I'm not sure it's that much warmer in Hungary than here."

He pushed open the door to the office. Christian felt a slight disappointment as Julia Nagy wasn't sitting at her desk.

Merton asked them to be seated. Then he went to his desk and pressed a button. "We'll order something to drink," he said. "How about an iced orangeade?"

"I wouldn't mind," Christian replied.

"The bell doesn't seem to be working again," the manager said hastily. "I'd best go to the kitchen myself. Please excuse me." The door closed behind him.

"Is it courtesy day or something?" asked Moore mockingly.

"What d'you mean?"

"Because people keep apologising to us."

"Oh, yes," Christian said absentmindedly. "Do you have a pencil, Moore? I'd like to make a note of something quickly before I forget it."

Moore looked at him in amazement. Since when did the boss forget anything?

He reached into his pocket and pulled out a ballpoint. "Thanks." Christian took the pen and wrote something on the back of his cigarette packet.

"How's your wife, by the way?" he then asked casually. As he did so, he turned the box so that Moore could read what he had written.

"CONTINUE TALKING!" it said.

"Oh, all right," Moore said. "She has a bit of a cold. Funny, actually, in the middle of summer. But you leave all the windows open because of the heat and you get the sniffles."

While Moore continued to talk about irrelevant things, Christian stood up quietly and went to Merton's desk. He put his hand on the button that Merton had operated earlier. Then he bent down. Sergeant Moore rose tensely. The grinding sound of a running tape recorder was clearly audible.

Christian pressed the button. The noise stopped. So he had guessed correctly: Merton hadn't rung for the waiter, but had switched on the tape recorder! Then he'd left them alone so that they could tell each other things that they wouldn't have revealed in his presence.

The door opened. It wasn't Merton with a waiter.

"Come in," said a young, fresh voice with a slight foreign accent.

Christian's head went up. "Good afternoon, Miss Nagy. I'm glad to see you." He stood up. He found it difficult to mask his embarrassment. Astonishment and slight suspicion crossed her expressive face in a matter of seconds. When she held out her hand to him, however, she was already acting impartially again. "Good day, Mr Stiller. Ah, and Mr – Moore?"

"That's right!" said Moore. "You have a good memory, miss."

"I wish it were worse," she said, turning quickly to the man who had come into the room behind her. "This is Mr Cooper – he's one of our guests. Mr Cooper, these two gentlemen are from Scotland Yard. So you can say whatever you like."

George Cooper gave them a friendly nod. He looked like a pensioned colonial officer. Taut and in good shape despite being at least sixty years old. Christian looked him in the eye and was amazed to see that it wasn't easy. Cooper had a bright, penetrating gaze that seemed to read behind his eyes.

"Mr Cooper's just complaining that someone searched his bungalow in his absence," Julia Nagy explained.

"Is anything missing?" asked Christian with professional interest.

"No," Cooper replied shortly. "There's nothing missing."

"Could it have been the maid?" asked Christian.

"Got her for the third summer now." Cooper's voice sounded dismissive. "It would be the first time she's done something like that."

Julia Nagy shook her head vigorously. "I'd stake my life on Bessie!" she declared energetically.

Christian smiled at her benevolently. Then he turned to Cooper once more. "How did you know the bungalow had been searched?"

"Because everything's all mixed up," Cooper said shortly. "My papers – my records – everything."

"You're a writer, I believe?" asked Christian, interested.

"A private scholar." The curt answer sounded as if he wanted to say: What's it to you?

"Mr Cooper's an Egyptian lawyer," Julia Nagy softened the brusque answer. "Did I pronounce that correctly?"

Cooper bowed. "Excellently." He didn't seem to be a man of many words. Yet Christian hesitated to classify him. Could it be that Cooper was playing a role? An unworldly gerontologist – with those eyes? But there was no way to sort that out now. "Do you want to press charges?" he asked.

"No."

Christian nodded. He wouldn't give Cooper another chance to let him leave.

But Julia Nagy spoiled his concept. "Then Mr Stiller can't do anything for you!"

"I had no intention of asking him to do that." That sounded so cutting that Christian gritted his teeth involuntarily. If Cooper was involved in this case, he was indeed a piece of work to cut your teeth on.

Christian noticed that Julia Nagy was looking perplexedly back and forth between him and Cooper. What had she said about Cooper yesterday? A scatty professor with whom one

49

could only talk about Egypt and Babylon? Had she deliberately told an untruth – or did she know Cooper from a completely different angle? That would explain her perplexity.

The awkward silence was broken by Victor Merton. He came in with a tray on which were two glasses and a cup.

"I shall have two more glasses brought right away," he said, pressing the button on his desk with his free hand.

Christian looked at him. "It's on again now," he said lightly.

"What?" Merton played the astonished man.

"The tape recorder," Christian said amiably. "I turned it off earlier because it was making such a racket. You could hardly stand it."

For a moment he thought Merton would drop the tray and just walk away. The glasses clinked together, so the manager of the High Dive shook. But that was probably only from the effort with which he controlled himself.

Merton put the tray down and slapped his forehead with well-played bewilderment. "What an idiot I am! I'd forgotten all about that! The tape recorder was only installed a few days ago, you know. No wonder the bell didn't work then!"

Christian looked at him with unchanging friendliness. "It's the heat, it gets to everyone at some point," he said. "That temperature excuses everything, don't you think so, Miss Nagy?"

Julia Nagy remained silent. Her half-open lips trembled. Her face was grey. Without the suntan it would have been deathly pale.

For a moment Christian met Cooper's gaze. A small, amused flame seemed to flicker in his bright, penetrating eyes. But that might be a reflection of the sunlight falling on the terrace outside. In any case, Cooper's voice sounded as icy as before.

"Don't you want to turn that thing off at least now?" he asked.

"Of course, sir." Merton reached for the button, pressed it.

"Where's the microphone?" continued Cooper.

"In the desk lamp, I suppose," Christian said. "Anyway, there's a branch off its cable, into the desk, of course."

They all looked at Merton, who seemed to squirm under their gaze.

Then the phone rang and made them jump. Julia Nagy hesitated involuntarily before picking up the receiver and answering. Immediately afterwards she handed it to Christian. "It's for you!"

Moore whistled through his teeth. "Our friend again, maybe," he said softly.

But it was Christian Stiller's secretary. She had only a brief message.

"I thought you would be interested. The house at No. 8, Dorchester Close, St. Johns Wood ..."

Mary Frederick's house – where Carol West had rented a room!

"What about it?"

"It's on fire, sir. The message just came. I thought..."

"Thank you," Christian said. "Yes, I am interested – very interested."

CHAPTER FIVE

The Attack

Christian Stiller put his foot down hard on the accelerator and the car shot forward. The gravel surface of the car park crackled. Then the dust of the country road blew behind them like a flag.

"It's madness," Sergeant Moore said quietly.

"What did you say?"

Christian had to speak loudly to drown out the engine noise and the whistling of the driving wind.

"I mean it's the craziest case I know," Moore exclaimed. "We've got a bunch of suspects – and not a glimmer of a motive."

Christian smiled grimly.

"I've infected you with my impatience, haven't I?" He overtook a truck and turned back onto the left side of the road in front of him. "Yet the case is only a day old. We mustn't expect too much, Moore!"

The sergeant looked at him, puzzled. Then he realised that his boss wasn't trying to urge him to be patient, but himself. But at the same time he was relentlessly pushing the scales forward. As relentlessly as he had been chasing himself since the murder of Carol West had to be solved.

"Do you think it's arson?" asked Moore, just to say something.

"It wouldn't surprise me," Christian replied. "Do you know Mary Fredericks?"

"Only from what you told me about when you spoke to her before. What she said sounded credible. Widow, alone in the house, rents rooms to working girls. That girl's name was Carol West and she was murdered last night – it could happen to any landlady."

"D'you know what her name used to be?"

"Mrs Fredericks? No, I don't."

"Mary Kenton. She was an actress. Not a famous one, but I saw her two or three times. Played pretty young thing parts with moderate success. Until she married – and probably got too fat for her trade. Or too comfortable."

Moore nodded. "The way she looks now, I don't think anyone will find her seductive."

He had to hold on. Christian turned to the right on to a narrower road. It was the shortest way to the north-west of the giant city of London.

"You talk about her as if she's still alive," Moore said between turns.

Christian took one hand off the steering wheel, fished a packet of cigarettes out of his pocket and put one in his mouth. Moore gave him a light.

"You're convinced she's dead?"

"Why else would someone set fire to her house?" the sergeant asked back. "I don't think it's an accidental fire. But if it's arson, then it's probably to cover up some sort of crime."

Ten minutes later, Christian stopped the car in front of a smoking pile of rubble that had once been a house. The fire brigade was still there. They limited themselves to protecting the nearest buildings from flying sparks. Christian got out and got a report from the fire chief.

"There's nothing to be done, sir," the man explained, hoarse from the smoke. "We were here six minutes after the alarm was raised. But the house was burning like tinder."

"Who alerted you?"

"The neighbours. They'd seen smoke from open windows on the ground floor."

"You only leave windows open on the ground floor when you're at home," Christian said.

"Quite right, sir," the fire chief confirmed. "But I still don't understand. The house burned so quickly that I don't ..." He hesitated.

"Don't believe in coincidence?"

"Yes, sir! It looked like the fire started in several places at once. If anyone was in the house, they could escape through the windows on the ground floor. So the owner of the house, a Mrs Fredericks by the way, wasn't in the house."

"Or she couldn't move," Christian said seriously. "How long will it be before we can search the rubble?"

"If we're allowed to put it under water: a day. But then everything in the way of clues will be destroyed. That's why you ask, isn't it, sir?"

"Yes," said Christian, "that's why I'm asking."

***

At closing time, Scotland Yard is little different from other authorities. Christian Stiller and Sergeant Moore struggled to get into the building between the stream of colleagues coming out. It was empty now – except for those on call.

"I hope the mug books are still open," Christian said.

"What do you need, sir?" the sergeant asked. "I could get whatever it is right now."

"I want to see all the files on Eddie Lombard."

"They should be on your desk already, sir. I ordered them at lunchtime today. When you told me what had happened at Lombard's this morning."

"Good thinking. Thank you, Moore. Now, if you could just get me something to drink, I'd be eternally grateful."

"Yes, sir. Something to eat as well? A sandwich or –"

"No thanks. Just a drink. I'm not hungry in this heat."

Five minutes later, Christian was sitting at his desk, leafing through the voluminous file. He was bored with the reports filed at the front. There was nothing in those that he didn't already know the basics of.

He was studying the photos when the door from the corridor opened. Moore came in with a pot of tea and two cups. "Leave the door open," Christian said. "It's suffocating in here."

He stood up.

"What's that?"

It was a thick business envelope.

"I found it outside. I wonder if it belonged to the Lombard files," said Moore.

Christian took it in his hand. No, it said "SUPERINTENDENT STILLER, PERSONAL". The address was simply "NEW SCOTLAND YARD". No stamp. So it was delivered by messenger.

Christian reached for the letter opener. The envelope was stuck tightly shut. He had to drill the tip into it.

At that moment, Moore looked up.

"Careful, boss!"

His face was contorted.

Then Christian also heard the hiss. Quick-wittedly, he hurled the envelope away towards the door. Then he ducked. Moore pressed himself against the wall. There was an explosion and the office windows shattered with a clang.

Then there was an almost painful silence. Christian looked at Moore. Thank God, apparently nothing had happened to him either.

A cleaning lady appeared in the doorway. "'Ere, what are you doing?" she asked crossly.

"I'm afraid I've given you some clearing up work to do," Christian said with a guilty look at the shards of glass and crumbled plaster.

"But please leave everything like that for now. I'll have to call the explosives people first."

"I don't think that'll be necessary," the woman replied. "If they don't come of their own accord after the noise, they must be deaf."

Her guess was right. Within minutes, everyone that was on duty at that time was gathered outside Christian's office. He said a few explanatory words and then retired to his desk. Only indistinct voices sounded through the door, which he'd closed behind him.

"It's a good thing all the windows were open," the sergeant said calmly.

"Indeed. And thank you for the warning. How did you think of that, Moore?"

"I saw a wire when you opened the envelope."

He put a full cup down for Christian and took the other. As far as he was concerned, the matter was settled. Christian lifted the cup and put it straight back down. The phone rang. He picked it up.

"Congratulations," someone said.

It was the man with the soft, polite voice.

"Oh, it's you again, my friend!" mocked Christian.

Moore understood and sprinted into the next room.

"What do you want to congratulate me on?" Christian continued in the same tone.

"For surviving the bomb attack, of course," he said back.

"Oh, you already know that?" Christian didn't need to adjust himself. The congestion in his voice was genuine.

"You hear all sorts of things," the other said without pride. "By the way – if you care for some advice..."

"But of course! Advise away." He had to hold the man on the line until Moore had determined where he was calling from.

"Take care of Robin Long," the other one said. Then there was a crack on the line. The caller had hung up.

Christian looked up. The sergeant was standing in the doorway.

"They're trying to track him down, boss. They'll get back to you in a minute. What did he want this time?"

"To congratulate me on surviving the danger. He also wants us to take care of Robin Long."

"But that – that means..."

"That he has an accomplice here in this building," Christian said quietly.

"But that's not possible..."

The phone in the next office rang. Moore went to answer it. Christian heard him speak.

Then the sergeant returned. His perplexity was clearly visible.

"It's not worked, boss!"

"What's not worked?"

"They can't trace the number."

Christian looked at him anxiously. He hadn't seen his aide this agitated in a long time. Was it just the sergeant's concern for him?

"Now sit down here and drink your tea," he said. "Don't let it get to you, you'll see that in the end we'll find a logical explanation for everything."

Moore sat down. When his cup was empty, he asked, "What are you going to do now, sir?"

"Take the advice I was given."

"Go to see Robin Long?"

"Yes. Get me the address of the hospital he's in, please. The station in Belhampton must have it. Also, put Lombard under surveillance. Send some detectives to his nightclubs, too."

"Today? That's going to be difficult."

"It has to be now. Besides, there's overtime and expenses. Let's say: exceptionally high expenses. On my say-so."

Moore smirked.

"That'll help. But what about the High Dive? Don't you want to have that monitored as well?"

"We can't. How are we going to hide people out there?"

"As guests!"

"I'd rather not. Anyone who moves in now is going to look suspect. Tell Belhampton to step up their patrols. That's all we can do for now. Maybe I'll look in again."

"Be careful if you do, guv!"

"One more thing, Moore. Yesterday you questioned Mr and Mrs Beckworth and that Mr Cooper. Did you write down their addresses?"

"Of course."

"Then have all three checked out."

"It's already done. The reports are on my desk over there. Beckworth really is a respectable merchant in Liverpool. Eve's his wife. Everything they told me seems to be correct."

"And what about Cooper?"

"The address is correct. He's been there for about ten years. His neighbours think he's a weirdo. No complaints, though. A friendly older gentleman..."

"Friendly is a good word."

Christian couldn't help thinking of his encounter with Cooper. He regarded the man as being as cold and hard as steel.

"Well done," he praised the sergeant. "We'll leave the Lombard file here, and please remember the hospital."

Moore nodded and went to make a phone call.

Christian looked through the photos attached to the reports on Eddie Lombard's activities. Most of them showed Tomato Eddie himself. At the beginning of his 'career', when he was still dealing in fruit and vegetables and had to be released for the first time due to lack of evidence. Then later ones that were never presented to a court because they weren't sufficient evidence. Then there was the Lombard of today. Bull-necked, thick-skulled, dangerous. I wonder if the envelope came from him. Moore came up with the address. Christian offered him a visitor's cigar.

"I've kept you here late..."

He waited until the cigar was lit.

"There's just one more question," he then said. "Forget for a moment that you are Sergeant Moore and that you are working with me on the Carol West case. Tell me: what makes me different from my colleagues? You know that the Yard has quite a few superintendents. You know just about all of them. Why would anyone be so persistent in trying to kill me? Why am I, of all people, so dangerous to him?"

Moore pondered for a moment.

"There's one skill in which you're way ahead of the others," he said. "You may not know it, but everyone admires your memory for people. Stiller is the man who never forgets a face. I've heard that said a hundred times – and it's true."

"Unfortunately, that's no longer true. Since yesterday I've been trying to remember why Carol West's face seems familiar. But..."

He looked thoughtfully ahead of him. His memory for faces could actually mean that someone feared him because he – because only he could possibly remember Carol West's face? But why him of all people? Why did one need a particularly good memory to remember Carol West? Because it had been so long since she had had any dealings with Scotland Yard? Nonsense! She was too young for that – and he himself, the youngest Superintendent of the Yard, was not responsible for old, forgotten cases. Why then? He closed his eyes and concentrated on this point. Why was Carol West so hard to recognise?

Suddenly the thought occurred to him: because her face had changed!

"Moore!"

"Sir?"

"First thing tomorrow, please: request a report from the doctor who conducted the postmortem on Carol West. I need to know if he found any traces of facial surgery. I also need her fingerprints. Have them cross-referenced with all available files. If necessary, send the prints to all Interpol members. Someone must have them!"

He stood up. "Now I'm off to see Robin Long, the teacher and suicide candidate."

***

He reached the small, modern hospital while it was still daylight. The doctor on duty raised his eyebrows when he saw the ID.

"You can see him but only for five minutes! He is still quite weak. And please don't upset him!"

Long was lying in a single room. His face was pale and gaunt and his breathing was laboured.

When he heard Christian's name, he narrowed his eyes.

"Oh, you're the man who saved my life!" He found it difficult to speak, but the hatred in his voice was unmistakable. "You think I should thank you, eh? The devil take you! You should have let me die!"

"I've not come for you to thank me," Christian said calmly. "I only want some information from you. I found a note in your room with my telephone number on it. What does that mean? What did you want from me?"

"I didn't want anything from you."

"Mr Long, be reasonable. Why did you write down my number? You must have had a reason."

"No, damn you!" shouted Long. A fit of coughing shook him and he struggled for breath.

A nurse rushed into the room. She assessed the situation with a glance and began to prepare an injection.

"You mustn't upset him," she said reproachfully to Christian. Then she stuck the needle into Long's arm.

Christian went into the doctor's room.

"It was no use," he said. "He raved and had a fit. The nurse is with him."

"He's a difficult case," the doctor confirmed noncommittally. "But suicides usually are."

Christian shrugged his shoulders. "He can do whatever he wants for all I care. But I have a murder to solve. I need all the support I can get."

"What murder? I didn't hear anything."

"The girl at High Dive."

"That was murder? All the papers said was..."

"The papers don't know yet. She was strangled. There was a phone number in her notebook. It was mine. Long also had the same number in his room."

The doctor looked at him with interest. "Is that so? Then I understand why the whole world's interested in him."

"The whole world? Who do you mean exactly?"

"I can't say exactly. But we've had ten or twelve calls from people asking about him."

"Was it always the same one?"

"The nurse said once it was a woman and otherwise it was men. But different ones each time."

"Was there one with a remarkably quiet, polite voice?"

"Yes. I even took that call myself. I just happened to be in the office at the time. The voice caught my attention."

"And a woman, you said?"

"Yes. I assume it was his sister."

"Did she say that?"

"On the phone, no. But afterwards, when she came here."

Christian leaned forward.

"What did she look like?"

"She was tall, slim and blonde. About thirty, I'd say."

Could it have been Eve Beckworth? Christian didn't doubt it: she had watched Long being taken away from the school. Then she had visited him in hospital. I wonder if she really was his sister.

"Was she allowed to see him?"

"We let her into his room as next of kin. But we shouldn't have done that. Within minutes they were shouting at each other. We had to throw the lady out because he was having a fit."

"What were they arguing about?"

"I don't know. All I know is that they were talking about a girl. 'She was your mistress,' she cried. It didn't sound very sisterly, I should say."

"Are you sure she said she was his sister?"

"I'm absolutely sure. That reminds me, by the way: The lady gave her name. Something with -worth or -work at the end."

"Was it Beckworth?"

"I believe so."

"Thank you, doctor, that's very important to me."

He stood up and stepped towards the window. It was almost dark outside. "She was your mistress," he thought. Couldn't that refer to Carol West?

"Doctor, I have a question. Would it suit a psychopath like Long to be constantly on guard over the morals of his environment on the one hand and have a secret lover on the other?"

"Quite," said the doctor.

Christian turned to him. "Would you think a man like that capable of committing murder?"

"Under certain circumstances, yes. I can't speak of Long, of course. But most murders are committed by people who are – roughly speaking – mentally unbalanced."

"I know. A psychopath is more likely to commit murder than a normal person."

"Far more likely. Which doesn't mean he's not responsible for his actions."

"But if..."

He broke off and listened. Somewhere a heavy object fell over with a thud.

Then a woman's shrill cries for help rang through the building.

CHAPTER SIX

A Strange Evening

The quiet of the evening was shattered. Doors were opened and hasty footsteps ran towards where the scream had come from. Long! With two movements Christian Stiller was out in the corridor. He listened, then he raced off in the direction he'd come from earlier.

Behind him he heard the doctor's footsteps. Robin Long! Maybe he was Carol West's killer after all. And now...

Again the woman screamed as if she was in the greatest distress. It must be the nurse who had stayed with Long.

Christian yanked open the door. The bed was empty.

At the window two figures wrestled with each other.

Christian jumped towards them. He grabbed Long's arm and turned him on his back. Long offered no resistance as the detective led him to his bed. He dropped and turned his face to the wall.

"He tried to throw himself out of the window," the nurse reported as she struggled for breath. "And from the third floor!" she added. It sounded like an accusation.

"Anyway, you saved his life," Christian said reassuringly.

The doctor struggled to keep staff and the slightly ill patients away from the door. "It's nothing," he kept saying. "Please go back to your wards. Nothing's happened here. There's nothing to be concerned about." Finally he returned to the room. He brought a burly orderly with him, who sat down on a chair next to Long's bed.

Christian waved the doctor to his side. "I suppose there's no point in talking to him now?" he asked quietly.

The doctor shook his head. "Absolutely not. Come on, we'll talk more outside."

"He can't stay here," said the doctor in the corridor. "We're not equipped to deal with such cases."

"You mean he needs to go to a mental hospital?" asked Christian.

"Yes. At least for a period of observation he has to go there. It's not an easy decision to make for a doctor. I may speak frankly to you, may I not?"

"Of course." Christian offered him a cigarette.

The doctor took a deep drag. "You know what our laws are. Suicide attempts are punishable in England. That's nonsense from a medical point of view, of course. I'll have a guilty conscience if I refer the man to the mental hospital. At the same time, I set the machinery of justice in motion. But if I don't refer him, he might kill himself after all."

He let Christian go ahead of him into the office.

"I understand your predicament," said the detective. "But in this case, you have no choice. In any case, I'll be glad to know Long is behind thick walls and barred windows. The man's not only a danger to himself, but probably to those around him."

"Do you suspect him of committing the murder at High Dive?"

"Yes."

"Then why don't you arrest him? He'd be fine in the prison hospital."

"Because I can't prove anything against him. It's not just the murder and the suicide attempts. There are also things that happened that Long couldn't have done."

***

This point preoccupied Christian on the drive to High Dive. If he guessed right, Carol West was Robin Long's lover. He'd strangled her out of jealousy or some such other mundane motive. Then he'd tried to end his life. So far, everything was clear. A nice round case that had to be solved with the help of the Beckworth couple.

But what did the attempted murders of him have to do with it? What was the West-Long case, so simple on the surface, to a gangster like Eddie Lombard? And who was the anonymous caller?

There were two possibilities. Either he was mistaken, and Long had nothing to do with the murder. Then that meant the killer was in Lombard's circle.

Or Long was the murderer – and his case was in some way connected to another crime. No, not in any way. It was Carol West. Through her face, which he couldn't remember. Through his memory of people that could be dangerous to Carol West's friends.

Who were her friends? Eddie Lombard might be one of them. And his aides. Also Victor Merton, Lombard's employee, the manager of the High Dive. He was a handsome man, more likely to be a ladies' man than a gangster. But the tape recorder in his desk had made him more than suspicious.

And what about Julia Nagy, Merton's assistant? She was a splendid girl. One could still sense the temperament, the cheerfulness that she actually had to radiate. But it was as if there was a blanket over her. As if she was afraid of something. That was it: fear. Was it for herself – or for someone else? For Merton, perhaps? He was a man women fell in love with.

And what about Mary Fredericks? I wonder if she was buried under the rubble of her house. It would take a full investigation to determine if it was arson. And whether Carol West's landlady had survived the fire.

Carol West again! Her murder had to be solved. Then came everything else.

Christian stubbed out his cigarette in the ashtray and steered the car into the busy car park of the High Dive. He drove it into a corner where the glow of the modern curved neon sign didn't reach. Then he walked around the building.

A cheerful noise came from the floodlit swimming pool. On the terrace, the colourful shades of small table lamps shone. Through the open windows of the restaurant, a somewhat jazzy saxophone sounded.

He glanced inside. Only a few couples were dancing. Most were outside enjoying the mild air of the summer evening.

A girl got out of the water. She ran out onto the dark meadow with long legs. A man followed her. The two shadows merged.

Christian had to think of Robin Long's complaints. The High Dive certainly left plenty of room for an unfriendly imagination. Then the two reappeared. Their silhouettes stood out in black against a bright window. They were detached from each other and made the movements of drying and dressing. They disappeared in the direction of the exit.

Christian paid no attention to them. He only saw the window. It was bungalow number three. Eve Beckworth!

Slowly he walked towards the bungalow. At the leisurely pace of a walker and without looking around carefully. That would only attract attention.

He stopped between the door and the illuminated window which was only ajar. Now he heard it clearly.

The desperate sobbing of a woman.

He hesitated. He hated such situations. But it couldn't be helped. He had to speak to Eve Beckworth.

His knock echoed through the low bungalow. Hall, living room, bedroom, bathroom. That was all the small building contained. He knocked again. The sobbing stopped and footsteps came closer.

"Who – who is it?" a woman's voice asked.

"My name's Stiller. I'm from Scotland Yard."

"Oh!" She said a few quiet words he didn't understand. Probably a request to wait.

There were footsteps again. Then he heard the sound of water running. Of course, she was washing her face. Too bad, the chance of surprise was gone but he couldn't help it.

She came back and opened the door.

"Yes, what can I do for you?"

It sounded controlled and cool. Was this the same woman who had just cried so hopelessly?

He followed her into the room. In passing, she took her sunglasses from the table and put them on.

"Forgive me, but my eyes are sore. I don't seem to be able to stand the sun."

She tried to smile. "But please, won't you sit down?"

"Thank you." He sat on a chair and looked around. "Your husband's not here?"

"He's gone for a walk." Her voice had an undertone he couldn't unravel.

"Well, maybe that's just as well," he said. "Mrs Beckworth, you can guess what I've come for?"

"About..." She hesitated and bit her lip nervously.

"About your brother," he said quietly. "You know everything. You visited him in hospital, didn't you?"

She nodded.

"Good," he continued, "then I don't need to explain much. My point is to find out the reason for his suicide attempts."

"Attempts? I thought..."

"He made a second one earlier this evening."

She was silent. Only her hands trembled slightly as if she had to suppress a tremendous excitement with all her effort.

"Did he – is he all right?" she finally asked. Her voice sounded brittle.

"Yes, he's okay – as far as one can tell in his mental state."

"You mean he's mentally deranged?"

That sounded almost hopeful. As if she had found a way out.

He blocked it immediately.

"No, not deranged. I believe he's fully responsible for his actions." He paused to let the words do their work. Then he continued, "But he is completely disturbed. As if he has experienced something terrible. What?"

She sat rigidly. It was seconds before she slowly shook her head. "I don't know."

"Didn't you talk to him about his troubles?"

"He – he didn't tell me." She clasped her hands together. "He just yelled at me. I didn't understand what he wanted."

"Did it have something to do with a girl?"

"I don't know."

"Did he mention any names?"

"I – I can't remember."

"Did he mention the name Carol West?"

"No," she said quickly. Too quickly. He was convinced she was lying and that she had been waiting for that question. That she knew there had been a connection between her brother and Carol West.

"I'd like to help your brother if at all possible," he said. "It could be that he's innocent of a serious charge. It could be that he takes his own life."

"Let him!" She shot up from her chair and shouted at Christian. "Let him kill himself! He can't do me any greater harm, the scoundrel!"

She stared at him with distorted eyes.

Christian raised his hand defensively. "Nothing can happen to him for the time being. He's under supervision now."

"Yes," she cried, "yes! You do that! Pack him in cotton wool! Guard his precious life! So that he..."

She pressed her hands to her mouth. Her glasses slipped and fell to the floor. She paid no attention. Slowly she turned away. Then she walked out with strange angular movements. He heard her throw herself on her bed. The dry sobbing of a crying fit shook her.

Christian got up and walked quickly to the door. There was no point in staying here. He would send the maid to her, or else a woman to look after her.

He yanked the door open and moved aside with a quick step. But it was only John Beckworth who had been listening.

"Your wife's ill," Christian said harshly. "You should take care of her."

After ten paces he turned. Beckworth still stood motionless, watching him. Christian shrugged his shoulders and kept walking past the bungalows, which lay silent and black by the path.

Over by the pool, the fun was still going on. More subdued now, because the very young people were gone. But splashing water and cheerful shouts could be heard all the way over here.

Bungalow number seven, number eight, nine – he still had the plan in his head.

Number ten! That was the bungalow reserved for Eddie Lombard! The boss. The owner of the High Dive. The deadly gunman and secret king of London nightlife.

The windows were dark. Christian kept walking but then he was literally jerked around.

Something had moved. In the dark room behind the window. Determined, he went to the door and knocked.

Nothing.

He knocked again.

Still no answer and there wasn't any sound. He pressed the door handle but it was locked. Hesitantly he turned away and walked on around the main building and to the entrance.

The soft light of the entrance hall fell on glass doors, mirrors and upholstered chairs. There was no light in the office. Christian walked in to the bar.

It was a small room. There were only six tables and six stools at the bar. Five were empty. Julia Nagy was sitting on the sixth. Christian pushed himself onto the bar stool beside her.

"Good evening," he said. "You still on duty?"

She stared at him, aghast, and forgot to answer.

"I seem to be something like the bad wolf in the fairy tale today," he said casually, watching her in the mirror. The dull light of the bar made her even prettier. Her bare shoulders shimmered softly.

"Why?" she finally asked, just to say something.

He turned to her and looked into her eyes. "I startled you, didn't I? I'm sorry about that."

She twisted her mouth into a very small smile. "It was stupid of me. I didn't expect..."

"To meet me here?"

"No, I – I mean – I ..."

She blushed to her shoulders under her suntan. Then she swallowed and said, "I was just thinking of you."

"Something friendly, I hope?"

She held his gaze. "I was thinking that it would have been nice if I had met you in a different place and time. There was a time when I would have been glad." She lowered her head. "Please don't ask me what I mean. I can't tell you anything."

He had to suppress the desire to put his arm around her shoulders and pull her close. She seemed so tender and needy. "If that's what you wish," he said hesitantly. "But wouldn't it be better if you had a little more confidence in me?"

"Oh, I have confidence in you," she said, "a great deal of confidence. In Scotland Yard, too. But it's – no one can help me."

Her pain was real. Christian looked at her sympathetically, though he didn't know what she was talking about.

"If there's anything I can do," he said quietly, "please call me at the Yard. There's always someone there. Even at night. I'll be right over."

She smiled with her lips closed. There were tears in her eyes.

He looked in the mirror and said in a changed voice: "What do you have to do to get a whisky here?"

She looked at him in amazement. Then she grabbed him and slid off the stool. "Just a minute, I'll get Jo. She just went into the kitchen because there was nothing going on here."

Victor Merton, who had been standing in the doorway, came in and let Julia pass him.

"Good evening, sir," he greeted politely. "I'm glad you're thinking of us even when you're not on duty." It was impossible to tell if he was speaking in earnest or if it was mockery.

"I'm afraid it's not quite like that," Christian spoke again. "I had business here."

"Did your visit concern the High Dive?"

"Only very peripherally," Christian evaded.

Julia Nagy came in with the barmaid. She sat down next to Christian again. Merton remained standing next to them. "This round's on the house," he said. "You don't mind if I buy you a drink, do you?"

"Are you sure Mr Lombard won't mind about that?" asked Christian mockingly. "Is he here, by the way? I had the impression earlier that there was someone at the window of bungalow ten."

"That's out of the question," Merton declared firmly. "I should know. Or did you book someone into number ten, Miss Nagy?"

"No," Julia said, "there's no one in number ten." She said it mechanically almost like a robot.

"Well, I must have been wrong then." Christian turned away quickly so Merton wouldn't see him reading the opposite in Julia's eyes. She was a bad liar.

"That's what my job does," Christian said apologetically. "With time, you see ghosts."

As they drank, he reflected. So there was someone in number ten. Lombard – or someone Lombard had kept hidden in there.

But what could he do? Without a search warrant – nothing. And no judge would give him a warrant until he could say what he was actually looking for.

"So here you are," said an unfriendly voice behind them. George Cooper had come in unnoticed. "And our friend from Scotland Yard is here again."

While Cooper swung himself onto a stool and placed his order, Christian wondered for the second time about Julia's face. He'd already noticed in the afternoon how perplexed she'd looked at him and the Egyptologist when he'd behaved so unfriendly towards him. Like a child whose parents are at odds.

He looked at Cooper, who even in the evening looked like a former colonial officer. His gaze met the bright, penetrating eyes. Again he had the helpless feeling that Cooper saw through him.

But then Cooper turned to Merton and said casually, "At least it's quiet in here."

The manager of the High Dive raised his eyebrows. "Did the noise bother you, sir? I'm sorry, but it's particularly noisy at the swimming pool today."

"Not as loud as my neighbours, the Beckworth couple," Cooper said wryly. "They're making a racket like they're the only people in the world. Having a little marital spat, I suppose."

Merton coughed genteelly. He was probably hiding a grin behind it. "They're leaving tomorrow, sir. Mr Beckworth told me earlier."

Julia Nagy looked up in surprise. "But his wife told me they were staying a few more days."

Cooper shook his head. "Normally they're really nice people. Well, they'll be hoarse tomorrow, judging by their volume tonight, and no mistake! At least then there'll be a bit of peace and quiet!"

Christian looked at his watch. It was approaching midnight. "How late are you open to?" he asked the manager.

"Usually until about two. Sometimes later if we have persistent guests."

Christian pretended to stifle a yawn. "Well, I don't feel so persistent, anyway. Well then, have a nice evening!" He gave Julia a friendly nod, bowed curtly to Cooper and let Merton escort him to the door.

Outside, the manager asked quietly, "Allow me to ask you a question, sir: was it murder?"

"Yes," Christian said. "Carol West was strangled before she was thrown into your pool here."

"Thank you, sir." Merton bowed. "And good night, sir."

"Goodbye, Mr Merton," Christian said with emphasis. Then he walked across the car park to his car.

He started slowly and wondered if he should park somewhere and walk back stealthily. But what could he gain by doing that? Watching the Beckworths' argument? It would be long over by the time he got back.

And tomorrow was a hard day. Maybe the most important one in this case. If Sergeant Moore found Carol West's fingerprints... He had to find them! They were the link between her past and the murder.

***

He turned into his street. The memory of the night before came back to him. The mugging by Denny Winters. The fight in the dark.

Was it conceivable they would try again?

The strong beam of his headlights illuminated the whole street. Trees and bushes cast sharp black shadows. There were a few parked cars but nothing else. It was like every other evening.

Then he saw a car pull up behind him. A shadow that followed him slowly. Without lights, it was gloomy and threatening.

Should he put his foot down? The surprise would be enough. By the time the other car followed, he would be around the next corner.

That was it! Turn the headlights off so he wouldn't be a target against the bright surface in front! Then foot down and off!

He reached for the light switch. It was ten more yards to his house. Then off he'd go.

That's when he saw a second car pull into the lane in front of him. A window was rolled down. He saw the bluish glow of a gun barrel.

He knew he was trapped.

CHAPTER SEVEN

The Next Victim

The pursuers' car edged closer to Christian's car. In front, a second vehicle blocked the road. The barrel of a pistol shone menacingly in its window.

Christian switched off his headlights, jerked the steering wheel around and accelerated. A second later, he slammed on the brakes. Before the car had even come to a halt inches from the door of his block of flats, the detective had ripped open the door. He threw himself through the bushes into the front garden, let himself roll, crawled a few yards further and took cover behind the stone wall. Cautiously he raised his head. A few yards in front of him the dark car was still blocking the road. Suddenly he was bathed in light. The other, the pursuer, had switched on their headlights. Now he shot forward.

"Stop!" A sharp voice drowned out the engine. "Get out and put your hands up!"

It was a patrol car! The car behind him had been a patrol car!

The engine of the other car howled. But the gangsters didn't turn to run. They turned towards the patrol car. Were they going to hit it?

No. The cars sped past each other in opposite directions. A shot was fired. And then another. At that speed, they could hardly do any damage.

Christian got up and squeezed through the bushes to his car. He drove it into the street, parked it and got out. There was no sign of the gangsters' car now. The police car had braked and was now slowly backing up. He heard the voice of the passenger, who gave the description of the fleeing car over the radio. "That's all. Over," the man said. Then he leaned out of the window. "Are you all right, sir?"

Christian patted the dirt off his trousers. "Thank you, yes, I'm all right. Thank you for your help. I only wish I'd recognised you sooner." He listened to the static on the radio. "Why didn't you go after him?"

"Orders, sir. We have to keep watch here. Besides, sending the message was more important. We even have the car registration number. I don't think they're going to get far."

Voices sounded from the loudspeaker. The driver turned a knob. The voices became clearer. They called out street names, numbers, neighbourhoods.

"We've got him!" someone shouted into the confusion. The others swayed as he gave the street and direction.

"Now he's turning right! Head for Soho."

A deep voice gave orders. The ring around the pursuers tightened.

Christian leaned on the roof of the patrol car. "It's nice to hear how other people work," he said. "Was this all prepared in advance?"

"Not exactly prepared," replied the driver from the other side. "But we'd been warned that something like this could happen. I believe your Sergeant Moore tipped off our inspector."

The hunt had reached Soho. The voices from the loudspeaker sounded more excited. Then several cars called in at the same time with the result that none could be understood. Only snatches of words came through.

"Blocked... Swerved... Can't get through... Leave the car... two men... House number seven-ten... Block off... Search."

Christian pulled his bunch of keys out of his pocket. "This could take a long time," he said, yawning heartily. "Ask your inspector to notify me when he has them. Thank you again – and good night."

**

The ringing of the phone dragged him from a deep, dreamless sleep. He switched on the light and looked at the clock. Eight minutes to five.

Again the bell shrilled. He picked it up and answered it.

"Good morning," said a soft, polite voice he recognised immediately. "You should take care of the High Dive."

"What for?" asked Christian sharply.

"The second murdered woman," said the contact and hung up.

For seconds Christian held the receiver in his hand. Then he dialled the number of the Belhampton police station. He was lucky. Sergeant Ingram answered.

"Listen, Sergeant," Christian said quickly. "I've just had an anonymous call. The man claims there's been a second murder in High Dive. Seems it's another woman."

"Hold on, sir," the sergeant interrupted him. Then, after a few seconds, "I've just raised the alarm. Do you want us to check it out?"

"As quickly and as inconspicuously as possible," Christian said curtly. "Let me know what you find. You still have my number?"

"The same one Carol West had with her? I do, sir."

"Good, I'll wait to hear from you!"

He jumped out of bed and was under the shower in no time. Hot – cold – hot – cold, until he felt somewhat fresh. But the clearer his head became, the more his thoughts circled around the one point: Who was the dead woman – if she even existed? While he shaved, he tried to think about the senseless, nameless fear that was weighing him down. The kettle was already boiling when he gave up the fight and admitted to himself that he was afraid for Julia Nagy. Afraid for a girl he hardly knew...

Finally the telephone rang. A strange man's voice: "I'm calling on behalf of Sergeant Ingram. He asked me to tell you that we found a woman next to the High Dive swimming pool. She's dead."

"Who?" asked Christian hoarsely. "Who is it?"

"I'm sorry, sir, I don't know."

"You didn't see her?"

"No, sir. I'm here at the station. The message came through just now."

"Then tell the sergeant I'll be right over. In the meantime, have him keep an eye on High Dive. Also all of the bungalows. Don't let anyone leave. Is that clear?"

"Yes, sir!"

"Thank you." He tapped the fork, waited for the dial tone and dialled Sergeant Moore's number. Impatiently, he tapped his foot until he heard the sleepy voice of his aide.

"Good morning, Moore. Sorry, to wake you at this un-Godly hour but our anonymous friend called me again. He reported a second murder at High Dive. I sent Ingram over from Belhampton. And it's true."

"Whose body is it?""

"I don't know. I'm heading there now. Send our people after me. Photographer, forensics and so on, you know the drill. Then go to the Yard and get me a search warrant for every room in High Dive. Then go to Eddie Lombard's house. Get him out of bed and find out where he was all last night. And check the logs. Remember we still need to know about Carol West's fingerprints - and Mary Fredericks' burnt house. We need to know if she's under all that rubble. That's all, Moore. Take care."

"Good luck, sir!"

Christian ran down the stairs, chewing on a sandwich on the way. The patrol car was still outside.

"You can go off duty now," Christian called out to the two policemen. "I have to leave. How's the car chase going on?" He unlocked his car and got behind the wheel.

"Nothing yet, sir," the passenger replied. "They're squatting in some hideout. Our people had to wait until it was light and until reinforcements arrived, but now we'll get them!" he added grimly.

"I hope so," Christian said and stepped on the gas.

He raced his car through the early morning silent streets. Pigeons flew up in front of him so close that he involuntarily ducked his head and a cyclist looked after him, shaking his head.

The sun was above the horizon when he reached High Dive. He parked the car outside on the road behind the hedge, so that he couldn't be seen from the house, then he got out and looked around.

He could see two, maybe three men in uniform, half hidden behind trees. They were walking towards him.

"Come on, sir. We left everything as it was," said Sergeant Ingram.

He led Christian to the pool. There was something lying on the grass to one side. It looked like a bundle of clothes. As they got closer, Christian realised it was a woman. For a moment he hesitated.

Then he walked towards her.

It was Eve Beckworth.

He was ashamed to feel relief while facing the dead woman.

"Is that how you found her?" he asked the sergeant doubtfully.

"Exactly the same, sir. Only she was all wet, as if she'd been pulled out of the water. That's how she looked, with her hair all stuck together. It's not like that now, but the dress is still damp."

"Did you find any injuries on her?"

"Not the slightest."

Christian looked carefully at the two yards of grassy ground that lay between the edge of the pool and the dead woman. Finally he bent down and felt the earth.

On the surface it was dry again. But underneath – wasn't that a damp trail leading from the pool to the place where Eve Beckworth lay? The kind of trail that would appear when someone crawled out of the water, dripping wet, with their last ounce of strength. As he stood up, he heard a window open. It was bungalow three! It was John Beckworth, who had just looked over at them.

Immediately the door opened and the short, round man came running across the lawn in his dressing gown.

***

An hour later, the picture had changed completely. Instead of policemen in uniform, plain-clothes officers dominated the scene. They searched the grass, knelt next to the dead woman and handled cameras and tape measures.

Christian Stiller sat on the terrace and stirred his coffee. Across from him, John Beckworth, George Cooper and Victor Merton were also busy with their cups. At the next table, a stenographer was taking notes.

"I note," Christian said with barely concealed irony, "that a dead body has been found here for the second time in two days and that for the second time no one has seen or heard anything. Neither the staff nor you gentlemen. Mr Merton assures me that he turned out the light in the pool shortly after two o'clock and that no one was in or near the water at that time. His statement is confirmed by the terrace waiter. Mr Cooper left the bar soon after me, at about midnight, and went to his bungalow. He saw a light in number three but heard no more voices. Then he slept until we woke him up – as did Mr Merton. You, Mr Beckworth, had an argument with your wife last night... It was a family matter you won't tell me about. Eventually, your wife retired to the bedroom, and you slept on the couch in the living room. This morning you woke up and found your wife missing. Is that correct so far?"

"Yes," Beckworth said. The other two just nodded.

A man in a postal uniform came to the table. He whispered to the stenographer. He pointed at Christian with his pencil.

"Excuse me, sir," the postman addressed him. "I've just heard from the cook that a Mrs Beckworth has been murdered here? ...has been found dead?"

"That's right," Christian said. "Is there something you want to tell me?"

"Yes, sir, I've just emptied the letterbox in the street. There was only one letter in it. I took a look at it. You don't have to think anything of it, sir. Out here, one man knows another, and there..."

"What about the letter?" Christian interrupted him.

"That's what I'm trying to tell you, sir. The letter is addressed to Mr Long, the young teacher over at the boarding school. But he's not there because he tried to poison himself with gas yesterday. I got that..."

"From the cook at the boarding school, eh? Yes, yes, I understand," Christian struggled to remain serious. "Is that all you wanted to tell me?"

"Yes, sir, that's all. Except that the return address on the letter says Eve Beckworth."

"Give it here," Christian said. "And thank you very much too." He looked at the envelope and then laid it down on the table beside him.

The man looked at him, puzzled. "Aren't you going to..."

"Violate postal secrecy?" asked Christian. "Not at the moment. Thank you!" He gave him a friendly nod and waited until the postman had gone.

"Should I not open it?" asked Beckworth, stretching his fleshy hand across the table.

"No," Christian said. "This letter will ... Yes, what is it, sergeant? Oh, hang on, I'm coming."

Sergeant Ingram waited until Christian was standing close to him. Then he said quietly: "I've been on to the telephone exchange, sir. Between four and five o'clock only one call was made from Belhampton. At ten to five. The call was to you!"

"Where from?"

"From here at High Dive!"

Christian took a deep breath. This was a surprise, though.

"Good," he said. "Now I need to speak to Robin Long. He was taken from the hospital to a mental hospital yesterday. Find out where and get him here by the quickest way possible! Is bungalow ten guarded?"

"As you instructed, sir."

"Then stay by the phone. See you later!"

When he returned to the table, Cooper and Merton had ordered their breakfasts, but Beckworth had shrugged it off. "Thanks, I can't eat now," he'd said. It sounded reproachful. As if he wanted to accuse the world of treating him badly. It wasn't the tone one would expect from a man who'd just lost his wife, more like that of an aggrieved egoist.

Cooper seemed to sense it too. "You must eat something," he growled unkindly at Beckworth. "You'll need all the strength you can muster today."

At the word strength, Merton's mouth twisted in derision. But immediately his face was polite and smooth again.

Christian looked at Beckworth. "One more question, sir: when you woke up earlier, did you immediately miss your wife?"

"No, not immediately. The door to the bedroom was open. I could see she wasn't in bed, but I thought she was in the bathroom. It was only when I couldn't hear any movement that I looked. That's when I realised she wasn't in the bungalow."

"What did you think?"

"I thought she must have gone for a walk."

"Then why did you run towards us with all the signs of terror when you saw us standing by the pool? Why weren't you frightened when you arrived and saw your wife lying there?"

"Because I saw her lying there!"

"From the bungalow? That's over fifty yards away!"

Beckworth moved his mouth. "I was using binoculars," he finally admitted.

"Would that be the same pair your wife took on her walk yesterday?"

"I – I don't know."

"Of course you know! Think of the coffee cup you threw at my foot yesterday afternoon to distract me! So that I wouldn't see your wife coming out of the woods!"

Beckworth put his finger under his collar.

The slamming of a car door sounded from the car park and hurried footsteps approached. Christian looked around and saw it was Eddie Lombard.

"Good morning!" he greeted. "I hear something's happened here again. Your sergeant asked me all sorts of questions, Superintendent. I don't think it's nice, so much mistrust between old friends!"

He pulled up a chair and sat down. "But let him ask me all the questions he likes. I was at the Peking Club until half past four this morning. A hundred or so people saw me there and can vouch for me. Then I took a taxi home. It was about five o'clock then. At six o'clock your sergeant came. To get away from here and back home in an hour, I should have needed a rocket."

He twisted his face into a broad grin. "Sorry. Am I interrupting something?"

"On the contrary," Christian scoffed. "Mr Beckworth here will be very grateful to you for the interruption."

Lombard turned his head and looked at the man sitting next to him. Beckworth returned the look with a cold stare of his pale blue eyes.

"Have you got him under the cosh? Or did his old lady do it herself, eh?"

"You bastard!" cried Beckworth suddenly. "You want to blacken me? To ruin me? You and your den of murderers here! No decent person should stay here! Who knows what else will happen here! I don't want to think about it..."

He tried to jump up but Lombard was already on top of him and slammed his fist into his face. He grabbed the falling man, pulled him up and punched again.

Then Christian and the stenographer held Lombard back. Beckworth sank limply to the ground. Lombard wanted to kick him with his foot but Christian turned, fell forward and threw the massive man over his shoulder.

He fell crashing onto an overturned table. He stood up, with bloodshot eyes.

Christian stood two steps in front of him and ducked slightly with his arms bent ready to fend off any attack.

"Come to your senses, man," he said calmly.

Lombard shook his head, dazed. His gaze cleared and instead of murderous rage, there was anger in it.

"What an idiot I am," he said, slumping his shoulders. "I didn't mean to do it." He pointed at Beckworth, who shifted with a groan. "He annoyed me!"

"My God!" someone said behind them.

Christian looked at the startled Julia Nagy with a smile.

"There's been a little disagreement. Can you bring us some water and a towel, please?"

He watched her walk into the building, swinging her hips with a grace that was certainly not rehearsed in front of a mirror. Then he walked towards the man with the black bag.

"Ready, doctor? What about her?"

"There are no external injuries," the doctor said. "She died of suffocation. Only the autopsy can tell us how."

"Was she drowned?"

"I would assume so. If only I knew how she could have got out of the water. It's all pretty unclear to me. Could someone have pulled her out afterwards?"

Christian thought of the mysterious caller, but he couldn't imagine him as a life-saver.

"That's not very likely," he said slowly. "But please would you mind taking a look at the man in that chair over there. I still need him to talk to him. The dead woman was his wife."

The doctor raised his eyebrows. "How's he taking it?"

"The man's as cold as a fish," Christian said. "He thinks only of himself."

The doctor went to Beckworth, around whom Merton, Cooper and Lombard were now standing.

Julia brought the water and left. As she passed Christian, she hesitated and stopped. "You've questioned everyone," she said quietly. "Except me. Wh-why?"

Christian looked her in the eye. Then he said just as quietly, "Because you wouldn't tell me the truth after all."

For a moment she stood stiffly as if he had punched her in the face. Then she turned and went into the main building. Soon Lombard and Merton retired to the office. Christian didn't mind, the man he needed was Beckworth. He was still sitting at the table in a daze, with a large plaster on his face. The doctor said goodbye. "It's not too bad," he said. "More the shock than anything else."

"Good. By the way, doctor, can you arrange for the postmortem to be done immediately?" He spoke deliberately loudly, watching Beckworth.

He opened his eyes and looked at him coldly. "If you need my permission: You may as far as I am concerned," he said.

"Then I will do my best." The doctor left. Christian sat down opposite Beckworth. Apart from them, only George Cooper sat at the table. The private scholar devoted himself to his breakfast with his usual appetite. The waiter came, brought Christian a coffee and tidied up the overturned chairs. When he'd gone, Christian said, "Mr Beckworth, do you feel up to answer my question now?"

Beckworth raised his head. "I've already told you everything."

"Not quite everything. Why did you have a quarrel with your wife last night? Was it about your brother-in-law?"

Beckworth didn't answer.

"All right," Christian said, watching an ambulance coming down the road to High Dive. "No answer can be an answer too." He drank his coffee in silence.

Two minutes later, a burly orderly led Robin Long to their table. Christian pushed a chair out of the way. "Have a seat, Mr Long. I'm afraid I have some sad news for you."

"You don't need to say anything!" Long sank down on the chair without holding it. "Eve's dead. They carried her past me when I got out of the ambulance."

His lips trembled and his hands twitched nervously.

"I killed them," he groaned. "Both of them. The only two people I ever loved."

CHAPTER EIGHT

The Face

Christian looked up at the orderly standing behind Long's chair. The orderly winked at him. Cooper bit unblinkingly off a piece of toast. Beckworth stared at Long in disgust. "You may have strangled Carol West," Christian said quietly. "But you weren't here tonight. So you had nothing to do with your sister's death."

"Yes, he did!" Beckworth pointed accusingly at his brother-in-law. "It's all his fault! Everything was fine until he wrote to my wife telling us to visit him here. Now I'm a dead man! I can't show my face anywhere! I wish I'd never met this cursed family!"

Long seemed to have heard nothing of this outburst. He only saw the letter lying in front of him. The last letter from his sister. "Open it," said Christian, "and then show it to me."

The young man tore open the letter with a jerky movement. His lips moved silently as he read. They were still moving when he stopped reading and stared across the paper into space.

The orderly took the letter from his hand and handed it to Christian.

It was a suicide note.

The letter of a woman who was married to a man who loved only himself. Who was afraid for her younger brother, who was always in trouble.

Then the last paragraph: "JOHN KNOWS THAT YOU KILLED THE GIRL. HE WANTS TO DIVORCE ME. HE IS AFRAID FOR HIS REPUTATION. HE ONLY THINKS ABOUT HIMSELF. HE WANTS TO BE RID OF ME. WHY DID YOU DO IT, ROBIN! I AM DESPERATE. I HAVE NO ONE LEFT. I DON'T WANT TO LIVE ANYMORE!"

"Is that her writing?" asked Christian quietly.

"Yes," Long confirmed tonelessly.

Beckworth held out his hand. "Let me see." He just glanced at the letter. "That's her writing all right." Then he pushed the letter back towards Christian.

He looked at him, puzzled. "Don't you want to read it?"

"No," Beckworth said coldly.

"Then you can go." Christian's voice sounded strange even to himself.

Beckworth stood up. He didn't look at the men. He walked with dragging steps across the grass towards his bungalow.

"He's a swine," Robin Long said bitterly. "But I'm a murderer. You should have let me die."

Christian regarded him thoughtfully. If Long didn't feel so sorry for himself, it would have been easier to feel sorry for him.

"How did you meet Carol West?" he asked.

"Here," Long said wearily. "Three months ago. I loved her from the first moment I saw her. And I guess she loved me too. She changed my life. Before, I was bitter and hated the whole world." He clasped his hands together.

"We met," he continued. "Two evenings a week, that's all she had time for. She never told me why. She acted very secretively. I thought there must be another man somewhere. I was jealous. I wanted her all for myself."

He was talking fast now as if he was glad to be rid of a burden. "I threatened to have her watched. I also lied to her that I had connections with the police. I said you were my friend, Superintendent Christian Stiller. I'd read your name in a newspaper. She laughed at me. But I'd even written down your number from a telephone directory. I knew it by heart. Why don't you call him, I said. She said she would and wrote down the number."

He swallowed. The memory overwhelmed him. Then he went on quickly. "After that, we only met once more. We went for a drive. Not to High Dive – she didn't want to be seen with me here. We drove into the forest. She'd checked the number. She said she could never see me again. I wanted to know why but she wouldn't tell me. We argued. I was half mad with jealousy. I grabbed her by the neck... And suddenly she was dead. At first I felt no remorse. Only fear. I brought her here and threw her in the pool. To make it look like suicide. After that, all I could think was: suicide! Until I realised that I had to die too. As atonement. Because I'm a murderer. And because I loved Carol West."

He ran his hand over his forehead. "Eve came here. I'd asked her to because I wanted to tell her about Carol. Because I wanted to tell her that now she never had to be afraid for me again. Then when Carol was dead, Eve must have realised the rest. She came to the hospital and told me off. She'd even watched me being picked up. You know the rest."

He was shaking as if in fever. The orderly took his arm. "Come on, time to go."

"May I take the letter with me?" asked Long.

"You can have it after the trial," said Christian.

Robin Long nodded wearily. "I'll see you there again, won't I?" Then he allowed himself to be led away willy-nilly.

"I've got all that," said the stenographer from the next table.

"Good, then you can go now." Christian didn't look around. He also dodged Cooper's bright eyes, which seemed to read into him.

"Aren't you pleased?" asked George Cooper.

"What about?" Christian felt a stale taste in his mouth.

"You've solved the murder. Quite a difficult case, actually, if I judge correctly." Christian looked at him. Cooper could have been his father. He was easily sixty years old. But you didn't think of that when you saw him. He was too lively and too energetic for that.

"That's not even partly true," Christian said coolly. "I don't enjoy putting people in prison. But that's not what this is about. Have you ever seen an iceberg? Only the tip of it peaks out of the water. That's the tip of Carol West's murder. It's been solved. But the bigger part of the iceberg is invisible."

"That may be so," Cooper said slowly. "But aren't I right in thinking that the invisible part of an iceberg is also the more dangerous. That ships don't shear at the top, but at the sharp edges that lie under the water. It's good to stay out of their way."

"I'll remember that." Christian stood up and bowed curtly. Even as he went into the building, he thought he felt Cooper's gaze on his back.

The office was full of cigarette smoke. "There's nothing like a good air conditioning system," Christian said as he entered. "Did you turn on the tape, Merton?"

The manager looked at him, aghast. Lombard grinned. Julia Nagy didn't look up from her typewriter.

Sergeant Ingram put down his notebook and stood up. "No calls," he reported.

"Then we'll make a phone call ourselves," Christian said. "May I use your phone, Miss Nagy?"

She pushed the phone towards him without looking at him. He sat down on the edge of the desk and dialled Scotland Yard.

In a moment he had Sergeant Moore on the line.

"Yes, everything's fine here," he answered the sergeant's question. He didn't look around. Even so, he knew that everyone in the room was eagerly awaiting his next words.

"No, it was suicide," he said. "Perfectly satisfied ... Eve Beckworth ...yes, she was Long's sister, that's why ... Long confessed to strangling Carol West. She was his mistress... All right, I'll be right back. See you soon."

"Then it's all over and done with?" asked Lombard. He raised his arms theatrically. "No more suspicion rests on this place?"

"Both deaths have been solved," Christian confirmed, "and that makes me superfluous to requirements here. Besides, I'm expected at the Yard."

***

"Do you think Lombard will fall for it?" asked Sergeant Moore.

Christian drew little figures on his blotting pad. "I'm not sure," he said. "But we can't miss a chance. Maybe he really does think we're so stupid that we're putting the case to bed now. Despite all the attempts to get rid of me."

"Which Long certainly had nothing to do with," Moore added grimly. "Is the High Dive still being watched?"

"Not any longer. I've sent Ingram home with his men. If we're going to bluff, let's bluff properly. Maybe that will make Lombard feel safe. The better to surprise him later. Do you have the search warrant?"

"Here – complete with signature and stamp. We can raid the High Dive at any time."

Christian took the paper. "What about this Cooper chap?" asked Moore.

"Opaque, like the others. But we..." The phone rang. "Stiller," he answered. "Yes, put the call through to me."

He covered the mouthpiece with his hand and said to Moore, "It's the fire brigade. This must be... yes, hello? Stiller here."

A deep male voice said, "I'm calling about the fire at 8 Dorchester Close."

That was Mary Frederick's house! "You're the chief fire officer, aren't you?"

"Yes, sir. We've cleared the debris. It was definitely arson. The fire was started in several places at once."

"Have you found the body of the owner?"

"No one at all, sir. There was no one in the house at the time of the fire. Thank God."

The door to the corridor was flung open and a police inspector in uniform rushed in.

"We've got them!" he shouted, buttoning his pistol pocket.

Christian eyed him calmly. "Who? The EEC?"

"Oh no, sir! The two men who tried to get at you last night! Do you want to come?"

"What for? You'll bring them in, won't you?"

"Not yet we can't! They've entrenched themselves and are shooting. They've already got one of our men. Come on, or the car'll leave without us!"

Christian stood up.

A secretary stuck her head in the door. "Are you leaving, sir?"

"Yes. What is it?"

"A call from the coroner."

"Come in," the Superintendent urged. "Wait a minute. What's he have to say?"

"He found traces of facial surgery on Carol West. The nose in particular had been altered. The written report and the fingerprints are on their way to us."

"Thank you. Moore, you take care of the prints."

"Can't I do that later? I'd rather come with you."

"The prints are more important. I'll see you when I get back!"

They dispensed with the lift and sped down the stairs. In the courtyard was a fully-occupied team car with the engine running. The driver waved at them and they jumped into the back. Christian slammed the door, dropped into a seat and closed his eyes. He pictured Carol West's face. It was pretty, young with a relatively broad forehead and a pronounced chin. Then he tried to think of another nose to go with it. Not the dainty snub nose, but a broader, more powerful one.

The momentum of a bend threw him against the door of the car. A car honked in annoyance.

Christian continued to think. She must have had a prominent nose. Otherwise the operation wouldn't have changed her face so much. He put a curved nose on her, a bent one ...

Christian came to no conclusion. He couldn't, not in that shaking, twisting, badly-sprung car. And not in the middle of London's traffic chaos.

But the thought wouldn't leave him. Again he put a face together. This time it was more believable. A memory came up. A trial. A name that began with Com- or Cum-....

A jolt threw him forward.

"We're here!"

They leapt into the street and orders rang out. The policemen disappeared into hallways. Christian felt useless. He felt as if he didn't belong. What was he doing here anyway?

A uniformed man approached him.

"Please continue... Oh, I'm sorry, sir. I didn't recognise you right away."

"Where are they?"

"Over there." The policeman pointed to an old five-storey apartment building. "In the attic."

"Thank you." Christian went in. It smelled of food and of burnt powder.

On the fourth floor he found the inspector. He pointed upstairs. "That's where they are! We can't reach them. They'll shoot through the door as soon as anything moves."

"Is there no other access? Through the roof perhaps?"

"It's too steep. We can't get to the hatches."

"Can't we lower them down on ropes?"

"And then hang in front of the hatch as a target?"

"No, of course. You're right."

As he considered shots rang out above and the stairwell echoed with their noise.

"Tell your men not to shoot!" he shouted upstairs. "We need them alive!"

"Then we'll have to starve them out," came back the sarcastic reply.

Christian put his hand on the inspector's shoulder. "Come on. There's nothing to be done here. Let's take a look from above."

They climbed out of a hatch onto the roof of the house next door. From here, the town was a forest of chimneys, television aerials and sloping tiled roofs, in between the steeply sloping canyons of the streets.

Christian balanced on a narrow footbridge to the next chimney. Now he saw the firewall – and the policemen watching the roof of the neighbouring house with guns drawn.

"Anyway, they can't get through here," said the inspector behind him.

One of the policemen turned to look at them. "Heads down! They're shooting out the hatches!"

Ducking, they advanced to the wall. The policemen made room for them. Cautiously, Christian raised his head.

In front of him was the ridge of the roof. There were chimneys, two aerials, footbridges for the chimney sweepers and a little lower, the roof hatches.

A head appeared in one. Shots rang out next to him, tiles splintered and the head disappeared.

Immediately afterwards, a hand appeared in the hatch, holding a pistol. Blindly, the gangster fired in their direction. They ducked. With a hard bang, the bullets smashed into the firewall. A ricochet howled away over them.

Then there was silence. Christian was the first to look over. Nothing was moving any more.

Should they dare attack? No, the risk was too great. Whoever got hurt here and slid off had to fall onto the road.

A reflective surface attracted his gaze. There was glass. A thick, almost opaque pane was set into the roof about two yards in front of the firewall.

"Do we have tear gas?" he asked.

"Downstairs," the inspector replied. "Shall I send for it?"

"As much as you can. That attic is big."

A policeman rumbled away across the gangplank. Christian waved the nearest ones towards him. "Close to the wall is a skylight. You shoot that when I give the order. Keep to the edge if possible. We need as big an opening as possible."

The men nodded and went to their posts.

They waited. At one point shots sounded from the house next door.

"There's no house adjoining on the other side, is there?" asked Christian.

"No, it's just a building site," confirmed the inspector.

Then came the tear gas. Hand grenades, but with a small explosive charge. Christian placed them on the wall in front of him. He took one in his hand, ready to throw. "Go," he shouted.

At the sound of the first shots, he bent over. The glass shattered.

"Not enough yet. Keep going."

More shots were fired, so fast the ear could barely distinguish them.

"Good," he said as he threw the first hand grenade. It disappeared into the dark opening. It hit the inside with a thud.

There was a dull explosion.

The next also went inside. Thick clouds billowed below the hole. The next one – and another – and the last one too.

Then he ducked as fast as lightning and wiped the brick dust from his face. There was more shooting from within and the policemen shot back.

Then the shooting stopped. Christian straightened up. A motionless figure hung in the skylight. A pistol came out of his hand. It slid down the roof and hit the edge of the gutter and disappeared into the depths.

"That's the first one," said someone behind them.

They saw the dead man being pulled inside. Then something moved in the hatch.

"Don't shoot," Christian ordered. He saw a handkerchief. "He wants to surrender," the inspector shouted. "We've done it."

Slowly, the gangster pushed his way out of the hatch. He used only his left arm. The right hung limply. A large dark stain stood out on his light-coloured shirt. He dropped the cloth then he straightened up with difficulty and came slowly towards them.

"Jimmy Graves," Christian said quietly. "Did more time behind bars than..."

The gangster stopped and gripped his injured shoulder. His vision was distorted with pain.

He staggered. Took two, three staggering steps when his foot slipped. Christian swung over the wall and ran towards him. As he fell, the gangster reached out to him.

Christian threw himself onto the ridge and grabbed it.

But he was a second too late.

***

"They're both dead," Christian said.

"Who were they?"

"Jimmy Graves and someone I've no idea about."

"Graves?" The sergeant shook his head in distress. "He specialised in banks, didn't he? Unless someone was blackmailing him, I don't know how he'd get involved in all this."

"Was Graves a Lombard man?" asked Christian.

"He was a nightclub man," said Moore. "In a different one every night when he wasn't locked up at the time. He would have run into Lombard often enough then."

A door rattled next door. "Wait a minute."

Moore stepped outside. Christian heard voices.

Then Moore came back. He waved a piece of paper. "The fingerprints. They're in the index. But not under the name Carol West." He looked at the note. "Barbara Cummings was her name."

"Cummings? Quick, Moore, get the file."

Excited, Christian jumped to his feet. He went to the open window and took a deep breath. The mild summer air didn't soothe his tension. Barbara Cummings. Now he saw her face clearly. Hers wasn't an important face. She was a minor figure – but in a major trial. In a trial so important that the public and the press had been excluded. Maybe two – no, three years ago.

He conquered his impatience. There was no point in making assumptions now. Moore had to come with the files any moment. Then he would put everything together. But he'd been right. Carol West alias Barbara Cummings was the link.

Now he knew why they'd tried so desperately to get rid of him. Of course, no one could know that she was back in England. The whole scheme would have burst.

The door opened and Sergeant Moore entered, a fat folder under his arm.

"Here," he said, putting it on the table. "The solution to the mystery."

Christian sat down at the desk and lit a cigarette. "Classified," he said, pointing to the stamp. "We were right."

Then he opened the folder and started to read.

Barbara Cummings. She'd served two and a half years in prison under the pre-trial detention settlement.

"There it is." He slapped his hand on the table. "Now we know what's behind it: espionage!"

CHAPTER NINE

It Comes To A Head

Sergeant Moore asked, "Do we have to inform the Secret Service?"

Christian Stiller pulled on his cigarette. "MI5 would be responsible," he said thoughtfully. "But we'd better just notify them – for the sake of holy bureaucracy! We have to go through official channels."

"Oh, my goodness," Moore groaned comically. "How long will that take then?"

"Well, first there'll be my message to Sir Joseph Simpson, our all-powerful boss. He's at lunch now. If I'm lucky, I'll catch him early this afternoon. He'll pass the message on to the relevant military authorities. They get the documents, listen to their experts on the subject and ask MI5 to deal with it. MI5, i.e. the military defence, receive the files, listen to the relevant experts..."

"For God's sake, sir, stop it. Something else could have happened by then!"

"Exactly! Besides, there is a danger that MI5 won't keep us informed of their actions. They'd observe the High Dive, scare away our game."

"On the other hand, it would be the most convenient way to get rid of the matter," Moore said. "We report the matter and don't have to bother about it anymore. Let the experts worry their heads!"

"Are you being serious?"

"No," Moore admitted. "Not after those fellows have tried to kill you three times."

Christian laughed. "We have a private score to settle with them, eh?" Then he added seriously, "But it's something else.

I ... But what's this?" He flicked through the files on Barbara Cummings.

Moore stifled a grin. He thought of the High Dive office. Of Julia Nagy, the girl with the dark, sad eyes. He was too good an observer not to have sensed how much the little Hungarian girl was bothering his boss. There was reason for caution. She wouldn't be the first spy to succeed in this way.

Christian was looking at the photos. "Here," he said. "Take a look at this." He reached into the drawer and pulled out the drawing he'd received in the post two days ago. The face of Carol West. "Would you believe it's the same face? A distant resemblance, yes. That's what's been bothering me all this time. But look at the long nose in the photo! And they've also changed the cut of the eyes. No wonder I didn't figure it out."

"What was she doing back then, anyway?"

"It was to do with the Blue Streak missile. You remember: it was to be England's long-range missile for nuclear warheads. The work on it was later stopped. But that wasn't foreseen at the time. In any case, Barbara Cummings belonged to a spy ring that was to procure the plans for this missile. Her task was to get the plans out of the country. But it didn't get that far. The ring was busted before she could take action. That is why she wasn't punished very severely. Afterwards, her employers, who are somewhere behind the Iron Curtain, changed the girl's mind and smuggled her back into England with false papers."

"Wasn't that reckless?"

"Actually, no. If she was careful and didn't get into trouble with the law..."

"And if no one checked her fingerprints..."

"That's right, then she could have stayed here undetected for years. We can assume that she was either supposed to connect to a new spy ring – or to a part of the old one that wasn't discovered at the time."

"D'you think she had the same mission again?"

"Probably. You know what they say – once a courier, always a courier."

"But there's nothing left on the Blue Streak missile programme. What do you think they were after this time?"

"Maybe the Blue Steel."

"It'll be over soon."

"Certainly, but nobody knew that three months ago. And Barbara Cummings was here for at least three months before she was murdered."

"And that's how we got her fingerprints," the sergeant added. "Actually, we should be grateful to Long."

"Well, let's not exaggerate," Christian said. "A murder is always a disgusting act, whoever's the victim. Barbara Cummings wanted to have a private life and she fell in love with Robin Long, of all people. That was a serious mistake for an agent. From that mistake comes everything else. But we're losing time. Any updates on Eddie Lombard?"

"Tomato Eddie's nightclubs are under surveillance. So far, it's been useless. The only advantage was that we could easily check his alibi for last night. It's true. He really was at the Peking Club."

"Good, then call the whole thing off. Make him feel safe. We can't risk him recognising one of our people and feeling watched."

"But if he escapes?"

"He won't. Haven't you noticed that no new guests have arrived at High Dive since Carol's murder – I mean Barbara Cummings' murder?"

"Yes, I know, but..."

"I don't think that's a coincidence. Have one of the girls in the office call and order a bungalow for tonight."

It wasn't two minutes before Moore was back. "You're right, sir. I was listening in. The answer was: all the bungalows are taken today!"

"Anything else?"

"There'll be some tomorrow!"

"So they're turning away all the guests, so they don't get any spit on their necks. But tomorrow they'll have room. That means tonight's the big night. Everything will be over by tomorrow. By the way, who did you speak to on the phone?"

"Julia Nagy, sir," said Sergeant Moore.

***

The engine hummed softly as the tyres whirred on the asphalt of the country road. Trees emerged from the darkness, moved past and stayed behind. The spicy, mild air of the summer night penetrated through the open windows into the interior of the car.

"That's a considerable diversion," Sergeant Moore said.

"It certainly is," Christian admitted. "But if we're going to borrow someone else's car so we won't be recognised, we might as well add the quarter of an hour and get to High Dive from another side. It's much too early yet anyway."

Moore looked at his watch. "It's ten past twelve. What time do you estimate we have to be at the post, sir?"

"One o'clock should do. They don't turn off the lights in the pool before then, even if no one's in it. And as long as the lights are on and guests are sitting on the terrace, nothing'll happen."

"Why are you so sure?"

"Because Lombard has no way of knowing if there are guards in disguise among the guests. He must be expecting that we have sent someone there."

They passed through a wood. Behind it, a side path turned off and Christian followed it. Slowly he let the car bump along in the rutted lane. After a few hundred yards, he switched off the headlights.

"If the map's right, we should be there soon," he said calmly. In the light of the rising moon, the trees cast long, uncertain shadows. The brightness was just enough to let Christian carefully find his way.

"One thing I'd like to know, sir," Moore said, smirking in the dark. "Did you deliberately arrange for us to arrive here just after moonrise?"

"Indeed – how else would we find our way through the forest?" asked Christian back, oblivious to the undertone of admiration with which the sergeant regarded his voice.

He parked the car in the shade and they got out of the car.

"Please don't slam the door!" admonished Christian. He looked around. "There's the road ahead. On the right, the bright glow is coming from High Dive. D'you have your gun?"

"Yes," Moore said. He reached under his left shoulder and adjusted the gun.

Christian laughed softly. "I only ask because I almost forgot mine." He stuck his head into the car and let the glove compartment snap open. The gun was wrapped in a rag that smelled of oil. He unwrapped it and put it in his narrow leather belt. Then he took out a heavy torch.

"So, armament finished. Let's go!"

They followed the edge of a meadow without leaving the shade of the trees. Slowly the noise from the High Dive became clearer. They heard a few bars of music, the shrill screech of a girl being splashed in the water and the slamming of a car door.

They'd reached the end of the clearing. Now as they felt their way between the trees Christian shook his head in annoyance as a twig cracked under his foot. He felt like a city boy playing at being an Indian. It was all so unfamiliar. Keep going! A few more steps! They could see the lights of High Dive between the trees.

"Hold it right there," he whispered to Moore. Then he scurried on, ducking behind bushes.

After a few minutes he was back. "This way!" he said.

Carefully he led the sergeant to a small hollow, its raised edge overgrown with tufts of grass. They lay down in it.

"Great!" whispered Moore. "Unless someone trips over us, we'll be safe here. That's bungalow ten up ahead, yeah?"

Christian adjusted the torch and jerked the pistol to the side where it would be less of a nuisance.

"Right," he whispered back, "the mysterious number ten. And over in number one the lights have just gone out. Mr Cooper's going to sleep."

He looked at the luminous dial of his watch. "It's not even one o'clock yet. We can take it ..."

He faltered. A sudden gust of wind passed through the treetops and leaves rustled. Immediately afterwards they were drowned out by long, resounding thunder.

Christian looked up. There was still nothing to be seen but clouds. Behind the forest, the moon came out. It shone with unclouded clarity. "I hope the storm doesn't come here," Moore said. "The weather report only said Cornwall was prone to thunderstorms."

"I know," Christian interrupted him grimly. "It's only four hundred miles from there as the crow flies. What difference does that make to a thunderstorm?"

"Or the weather service," Moore added sympathetically.

"There!"

Again there was thunder. It was louder this time. A few people got out of the pool and ran for their clothes. On the terrace, where only a few couples were still sitting, there was also a commotion. Someone called for the waiter in a loud voice.

Ten minutes later, the changing room and terrace were empty. Cars turned onto the country road and quickly disappeared in the direction of the town. The band had also stopped playing. Probably the guests inside were leaving as well.

A man stepped out onto the terrace and looked up at the sky. A few wispy clouds passed over the moon and the trees were moving more briskly.

"Isn't that Merton?" asked Moore quietly.

The man passed in front of a window. Now they recognised him clearly. Yes, it was Victor Merton, the manager of the High Dive.

He went down to the lawn and took a walk around the pool. Then he returned to the main building. Immediately the lights of the pool went out.

They waited. The lights in the restaurant also went out. One last car left.

When the first heavy drops of rain fell, High Dive was in complete darkness.

"Now we're ready to go," Moore remarked redundantly. Probably just to say something at all. Christian also felt uneasy. He looked up doubtfully at the last remaining source of light – the moon. A heavy cloud was moving towards it. It looked as if a huge, dark hand was reaching for the shining disc in the sky.

He'd calculated everything so beautifully. The full moon also had its role to play: to rise in time and illuminate the scene. The thunderstorm had spoiled everything.

Now the moon disappeared. Immediately afterwards, a drumming curtain of water descended over the High Dive. Twitching lightning woke up short-lived, uncertain shadows. Crashing thunder made all listening pointless.

Christian thrust the torch into Moore's hand.

"Put that thing under your jacket..." He waited until the thunder had died down. "And follow me!"

He stood up. Moore followed his example. "Where to?"

"To number ten," Christian replied.

They took a few steps under the dripping trees. The next flash of lightning revealed the direction.

Then Christian ran off, feathering on his tiptoes, quietly and quickly.

A flash of lightning. There was the bungalow! Christian tried to stop but his momentum carried him to the wide window. It was open.

A shadow moved across!

Quickly! Before the other could act. The lightning went out.

In the crack of thunder, Christian swung himself into the room and immediately threw himself to the side.

But he was a little too late! The blow grazed his head and almost deafened him.

With weak knees he came up and saw the shadowy figure in the reflection of the next flash. He saw it lunge to strike.

He tugged at his gun but he couldn't get it out in time. "Hands up!"

Suddenly the room was bright. Sergeant Moore stood at the window. In one hand, the torch. In the other, his shiny service pistol.

Both were pointed at Christian's opponent.

On Julia Nagy.

For a moment she stood frozen. Then her hands opened as if all strength had left her. The heavy stool she had been holding fell to the ground.

Dazzled, she turned her face away. But the relentless beam of the handheld spotlight wouldn't let her go.

"Shoot now," she said. Her voice sounded breathless. "No one will hear."

She lifted her face into the beam. Her eyes were closed. It looked rigid like a mask.

"Shoot, I said!" she suddenly shouted.

"My God," Christian whispered, "that's ..."

He walked hesitantly towards her.

Then he jumped at her and pulled her to the ground.

Before the gunman at the door could pull the trigger a second time, Sergeant Moore fired. Wood splintered. Three, four, five times.

Then finally the beam of the lamp found the door.

Christian saw a shadow. He fired. He knew at the same moment that he'd missed.

"Lights out!"

Moore obeyed.

Christian tiptoed to the door. Someone moved in front of him in the hallway. Then a cold draught hit him. He jumped forward. In front of him the door slammed shut.

"Moore, the window!" he called sharply. He heard the sergeant in the room change position. Then he groped for the latch so, from this side they were no longer threatened with surprise.

The shots were almost drowned out by the rumble of the thunder. There was a bright bang. Then the muffled answer of Moore's heavy pistol.

"What is it?" he asked quietly from the doorway of the room.

"Nothing," Moore replied. "The devil should try and hit something in this darkness. But we're pretty much trapped, sir."

"Mr Stiller?" asked a soft voice from the corner of the room.

"Stay down, Miss Nagy!" he ordered. "You still got the torch, Moore?"

"Here, sir."

In the reflection of a flash he saw Moore's outstretched hand. He took the torch and went towards the other door he'd seen earlier. "What's behind the next door here? The bedroom?"

He heard Julia Nagy move.

"Yes," she said hesitantly, "but – I ..." She didn't speak any further. He pushed down the handle and pushed open the door. There was no draught which meant that the window was closed. The scent of a heavy, sweet perfume hung in the air. It wasn't Julia's. But it still seemed familiar to him.

He closed the door behind him and flashed the torch. There was a double bed, bedside tables, a dressing table, a built-in wardrobe – but nothing special. Thick curtains hung in front of the window. So there was no danger of him being seen from outside.

The wardrobe door was open but there was nothing to see – except empty hangers. But there was a silk scarf in one corner. As if someone had forgotten it during a hasty departure.

What was that at the back of the wardrobe? A black line? No, it was a wire. An insulated blade that came out of a gap between two boards and disappeared again between them.

It was trapped! Someone had closed a door or a flap. Probably in the dark... He found the opener disguised as a nail. A piece of the back wall flipped out.

In front of him was a radio. That was the secret of number ten! He'd been right. This was where it all came together. In this bungalow. Of course it was about spying. And Julia Nagy was in the middle of the net.

He turned off the torch and went back into the other room.

"Sir?" asked Moore from the window.

"Yes. What is it?"

"The rain's letting up, sir. Can you hear? The thunder's getting quieter, too."

Christian listened for the rumble of the departing thunderstorm. He had to make a decision quickly, or the birds would fly out.

"Miss Nagy, does the phone here have an outside line?"

"Only through the office," she answered quietly. "I have to give you ..."

"Sir!" Moore's voice sounded strained. "The flat shed behind the main building. Isn't that a garage?"

"Yes," Julia answered in Christian's place. "Mostly there's just a car in there. It belongs to Lombard. But he rarely uses it."

"He's using it now, anyway," Moore stated dryly.

"Then we must get there," Christian decided. "He mustn't get away from us!"

"Don't go!" pleaded Julia. "It's ..."

Over there, an engine started up. "Cover fire!" ordered Christian. Then he swung out of the window and zigzagged towards the house. He ducked behind the corner and pushed his head forward. No shots were fired. Had no one seen him?

The moon shone faintly between wisps of clouds. But its light was enough. Christian saw the dark mass of a car pushing backwards out of the garage and turning.

He sprang forward and raised his pistol. At that moment, the headlights flashed on. He stood bathed in light.

A bullet passed close to his head. The next one grazed his arm. He felt a searing pain and threw himself back behind the corner of the building.

Moore fired from the bungalow.

A bullet struck metal and the engine howled.

Was it too late? No, not yet. Christian turned and ran along the side of the building. Maybe he could get to the exit in time. Maybe he could at least avoid a few bullets from a distance.

A new series of shots rang out from the bungalow.

Why was Moore still shooting? Hadn't the others left yet? They should have disappeared behind the building long ago. Out of range of Moore's gun and regardless of the danger, Christian turned the corner and ran further. The entrance and car park of the High Dive were in front of him. But still no car!

It was getting brighter. No more clouds in front of the moon which was all the better.

Christian stopped before the next corner. Pressed tightly against the wall, he pushed forward. Then he saw the burning car. In front of the garage where he'd last seen it. They fled into the main building as fast as they could. He ran back the way he came. He wanted to force the door open with a kick. It gave way. It wasn't locked. He pushed it open and stood in the hall. Here at the side were the switches. He found them and pressed them down with the flat of his hand. The neon lights flickered on. First the one above him, then in the cloakroom and then in the stairwell. Then a violent jolt threw him forward. A bullet hissed past his ear. He let himself roll as he jumped to the side and stumbled across the carpet. He fell on his injured arm and a sharp pain paralysed him for seconds. Instinctively, he dodged the next bullet, which shredded the carpet in front of his face.

There was no third shot.

Christian jumped up and raised his pistol. But he didn't shoot.

CHAPTER TEN

Bungalow Ten

Christian Stiller couldn't shoot. He saw Eddie Lombard's bruised face and the smoking gun in his hand. And on that hand, on that arm, hung Julia Nagy, fighting fiercely like a wildcat. That was the reason why Lombard hadn't fired the third shot.

Lombard tried to shake her off. But she clung to his wrist. She wouldn't let go. Not even when he struck with his other fist.

Christian hesitated. He couldn't find a target. He was about to lunge at the fighters and grab the man's other arm when the door was pushed open once more. It was Sergeant Moore! And with an iron grip he led a woman in front of him.

It was Mary Fredericks. Christian's memory worked like a flash. The heavy, sweet perfume in the bedroom of bungalow ten. In the room where he'd discovered the radio. Now he knew where he remembered it from. From his visit to Mary Fredericks, the landlady of the murdered Carol West.

With a mighty jerk, Lombard hurled Julia Nagy aside. But he had no chance. He stood between Christian and Moore and was hopelessly off-balance at that.

"What's going on here?" asked a sharp voice.

Involuntarily, Christian turned his head. Without thinking he instinctively jumped to one side and fired. Lombard grabbed his shoulder. Once more he raised his gun with a distorted face.

That's when Moore's karate blow hit him in the neck. Lombard fell forward to the ground and Moore knocked his pistol aside with his foot.

Christian turned around. On the landing stood Victor Merton. He was wearing a dressing gown, the legs of his pyjama bottoms peeping out from underneath. He was pointing the barrel of a heavy, ancient drum revolver at Lombard.

"Put that thing away," Christian ordered. "And help us get your esteemed employer to the office."

Merton obeyed. He carefully placed the gun in an alcove. Then he came down the stairs, tightening the belt of his dressing gown as he did so. Together with Moore, he carried Lombard into the office. Christian followed with the deathly pale Mary Fredericks. He stopped at the door and waited for Julia, who followed with her head bowed.

"Thank you," he whispered as she passed him.

She didn't respond. With dragging steps she walked to her desk and sat behind it. Then she watched impassively as Merton took bandages from the medicine cabinet and the sergeant tore open Lombard's shirt and applied an emergency bandage.

Eddie Lombard had long since regained consciousness. Christian saw it in the twitching of his eyelashes, but the owner of the High Dive seemed to prefer to play the unconscious man for the time being. He only moaned softly as the sergeant tightened the bandage.

Christian picked up the phone. But the earpiece remained silent. The cable was hanging loose. Someone had ripped it out of the wall by force.

Moore straightened up. "There, that's him taken care of for now. Have you called the Yard yet, sir?"

Instead of answering, Christian showed him the torn cable.

"Oh, I see our friend thought of everything," said Moore, looking unkindly at Lombard. "But it doesn't matter. I'll stand in the road and stop a car. Or shall I go over and wake up old Cooper?"

Christian went to the window and opened it wide. Bungalow number one was still in darkness. George Cooper had to be a good sleeper.

"That's a possibility," Christian said. "We might also ask Mr Merton to get dressed and go for us. You'd certainly go to Belhampton for us, wouldn't you, sir?"

Victor Merton bowed slightly. "Of course, Superintendent, it is the duty of every citizen to be of assistance to the police. If you would only tell me first what my – I mean, what Mr Lombard has done. I can't think of him as – a criminal."

"Criminal's good," Mary Fredericks flared up. "He kidnapped me and kept me prisoner. And only because I wanted to know what happened to Carol West. As if I didn't have the right to be a little curious. After all, Miss West was my lodger. You can ... "

"Wait a minute," Christian interrupted her, "You mean Lombard kept you a prisoner here in bungalow ten? How long for?"

"Since the day before yesterday. No," she corrected herself, "it's already past midnight. So for over two days now."

"How did he get hold of you?"

"I went to see him after you came to see me. I knew him from when I was an actress. I knew the High Dive was his. That's why I let him drive me out here. Out of greed, and because I felt sorry for poor Carol West. But instead of taking me to the restaurant, he dragged me to the bungalow. I was terrified."

"Did he tie you up?"

"No, he injected me with something. After that it was as if I had been taken prisoner. I was completely without my own free will. It was excruciating. It was only tonight that I got better. Then Lombard came and dragged me to the garage in that terrible thunderstorm. He pushed me into the car and then there were the shots. I just ran away. Until your sergeant grabbed me and brought me back here."

She slapped her hands in front of her face. The memory of the excitement of the last few days seemed to overwhelm her. Christian gave Moore a questioning look. The sergeant raised his shoulders. "It could be true," he said.

"Do you know that your house was set on fire?" asked Christian. Mary Fredericks dropped her hands and stared at him in horror. "My house was? But why? Why does he pursue me with such terrible hatred?" she cried sadly.

"Probably he wanted to camouflage your disappearance. But let me ask you one more question: did you see anyone else in the bungalow apart from Lombard? Maybe someone who is present here?"

She turned her head and looked first at Merton, then at Julia Nagy. "No," she then said helplessly, "I don't remember anyone."

"Did you notice anything unusual in the bungalow?"

She looked at him uncomprehendingly.

"An unusual technical installation perhaps?" he helped her.

Then Lombard's eyes snapped open. "Oh, so you found my radio?" he asked with a sneer. "Tough snoopers you are at the Yard."

"Well, well, well." Moore paid him back for the sneer. "Our dead man can suddenly talk again, can he?"

Lombard shot him an angry look from the corner of his eye. Then he turned to Christian and said, "It's true. I locked her up. She was too noisy. The radio's mine too. Now get me to a hospital. My shoulder hurts."

Thoughtfully, Christian looked around the room. Mary Fredericks and Victor Merton were staring at Lombard as if his mere presence would taint them. Julia looked in front of her and – yes, hadn't she just shaken her head ever so slightly? Was she trying to warn him?

Lombard cleared his throat. "Lucky," he said hoarsely, "lucky that my father doesn't have to live through this."

Christian listened. Why did Lombard use the word father so conspicuously? Why did Julia flinch at that word? Was it a warning from Lombard to her? But what was behind it?

Christian sensed an unknown danger. If he sent Moore for the car, he was all alone here. Was that what Lombard wanted to achieve? But how could the wounded man be dangerous to him?

He walked over to Lombard and ran his hands along his body. No, the gangster didn't have a weapon secreted upon him. And yet…

"No," he said aloud. "I'm sorry, but we have to stay here. Mr Merton, when will your staff start arriving?"

The manager looked at the wall clock. "In about three hours the cleaners from Belhampton will be here."

"Then we'll wait that long," Christian decided.

Merton went to the open window, yawning, and sat on the sill. "It's cooled down after the thunderstorm," he said casually, wrapping himself more tightly in his dressing gown. That was the danger. But Christian was too late. Merton's hand reappeared holding a flat pistol, the muzzle of which was pointed at Christian's chest.

"Don't move," Merton said coldly. "Put up your hands. But slowly. Nice and slowly."

So Merton was Lombard's aide after all. And what a bluff, running up to his room, changing and coming down the stairs seemingly unaware. And now, after Moore couldn't get away, the final move. Merton pursed his mouth.

"You've done us enough damage since that mad Long put you on our trail. But now it's over. Mary, take the pistols from those two. The Superintendent has his in his trousers, if I saw right."

Christian blushed with shame as Mary Fredericks took the gun from him. She'd duped him. She'd played him for a fool.

Oh, sure, he'd never quite trusted her. Still, he'd been as careless as a beginner. He should have known that trained spies know more tricks than everyday crooks.

"So, now the other one," Merton ordered. "Yes," he ordered. A new suspicion flashed through Christian's mind. Was Merton, disguised as Lombard's employee, really the boss of the ring?

"Give me one of those things, Mary," Lombard said behind him.

He picked up the gun and let the safety catch snap back. "Close the window, Merton. No one needs to hear if there's a bang. And then let's get out of here. We've got a long way to go."

"On foot?" Merton looked at Christian. "Where did you leave your car? Do you want to save your life? If you tell me where your car is, we'll leave you tied up in the woods. If not – you heard Lombard."

An armchair groaned behind Christian. Lombard stood up. "Don't do anything stupid," he said. "Otherwise we'll have them on our backs again in a few hours. Close the window. You don't need to get your hands dirty. I'll take care of them. All three of them." He slammed the gun down on the table in front of Julia. "Yes-yes, all three of them. Even our little traitor here. You bitch." He punched her in the face. Her head flew back and blood trickled from the corner of her mouth. She didn't wipe it off.

Christian clenched his teeth so hard they hurt.

"Stop that!" ordered Merton sharply. "I'm the boss here. Save your fits for later, Lombard."

Reluctantly, the gangster obeyed. He returned to his seat and disappeared from Christian's field of vision. So Merton really was the boss. And he was a good actor, too.

"What is it?" asked Merton. "Where's the car?"

Christian hesitated. He was trying to buy time for one last desperate attack on....

"Speak," Merton ordered. "Answer me! And quickly. And don't move. Lombard, watch out behind him."

Christian had a bitter taste in his mouth. "What guarantee do I have that you won't kill us anyway?" he asked.

"None. None at all," Merton replied coldly. "You'll just have to risk it, won't you. Well?"

"Don't say anything, sir," Moore pleaded, "they're playing us so – why..." He faltered and collapsed.

Lombard rubbed the barrel of the pistol against his jacket. "That was quite a blow," he said with satisfaction, "considering I had to use my left hand..."

"Don't talk," Merton said coldly. "We haven't time for playing gangsters."

"Ah, being a spy's a better thing, I suppose?" cried Lombard. "I was good enough to do your dirty work for years. I couldn't be gangster enough. But now that you're in for it, I'm suddenly to blame."

"That's what you are. You spoiled everything with your idiotic attempts to have Superintendent Stiller murdered. That's what brought him to our attention in the first place."

"I had to prevent him from recognising Carol. He has the best memory in the Yard. But you – you couldn't even stop that lunatic from dumping Carol here at High Dive. That's how it all got out. You master spy, you. I want to..."

He broke off, staring dumbfounded into the muzzle of Merton's pistol. "Damn, I know you're capable but you won't really shoot me."

He turned and dropped into the armchair. "Get me a whisky, Mary. Out of the back of the bar."

Christian heard her footsteps. This was time gained. Time for the tape to run. Good thing he had pressed the button when he came into the room. In a few hours his colleagues would find the tape – and what was left of the three of them.

He felt Merton's gaze and said hastily, "There's a clearing in the forest behind the bungalows. Go along the right edge up to a single clump of trees. There – behind is the car. It's close to a dirt track."

Merton looked at him suspiciously. Christian lowered his eyes as if ashamed of his words.

"Good, you're being sensible at last," Merton said. "Lombard, get the car."

"First I want the whisky," Lombard protested. "I'm wounded. My shoulder."

Merton hesitated. "We need to get a move on. The motorship for Prague leaves Croydon at six. We must be there in good time before then. Are your passports and tickets in order?"

"Of course," Lombard grumbled.

Julia Nagy motioned. "Christian?" she asked quietly.

"Shut up," Lombard yelled at her.

Merton continued in an indifferent voice: "It's all right, you may speak to the Superintendent, Miss Nagy."

Christian turned his head and smiled at her encouragingly.

"My father," she said, "I did it because of my father. He's in Budapest. In prison. He's been there since the uprising. Merton knew and he threatened that if I hadn't helped him, they would have killed my father..."

Christian nodded in understanding.

"I had to do it. You must believe me," she continued. "I didn't do any of the spying. But I took calls and passed them on to Merton. I took letters to the post office with false return addresses on them. I didn't know there was a radio in bungalow ten." She looked at Christian in despair.

He smiled. "Go on."

"I knew Mary Fredericks was hiding in number ten."

"How did you get into the bungalow tonight?"

"I was hiding, too. I guessed the three of them were trying to escape. I knew they wouldn't leave me alive. You saved me, Christian. But what good does that do me now? I lied to you. I knew Merton was a spy. I knew that Lombard and Mary Fredericks were his helpers... That he paid them off. I've ..." She couldn't continue. There were tears in her eyes.

"I would so much have liked to tell you the truth, Christian." She swallowed and then she said bravely, "They will kill us. But first I have to tell you something..."

She listened. Footsteps were coming closer. It was Mary Fredericks with the whisky. Christian didn't turn to look at her. Instead he looked at Julia while a glass was placed on the table behind him and the whisky gurgled and flowed into it.

Suddenly Julia made a movement. He followed her gaze.

Merton was still sitting on the window sill. His legs were hanging into the room. But his posture was strangely stiff. His eyes were fixed. His pistol...

The pistol trembled in his hand. Then Christian heard the voice. He recognised it immediately. A soft, polite voice. It was the voice of the anonymous caller.

"Open your hand, and drop it," the voice said. There was something compelling about it. Christian was tempted to open his own hand. He saw Merton's index finger detach itself from the trigger guard.

Then he threw himself around and struck out. His fist crashed into the corner of Lombard's chin. The massive skull hit the wall. Lombard sank from the chair. Mary Fredericks wanted to jump up but suddenly Sergeant Moore stood in front of her and pushed her back into the chair.

Their pistols were on the table. As if on command, they reached for them and wheeled around. It was no longer necessary. Merton sat in the window with his hands up. His eyes were narrow black slits.

"Get down!" ordered Christian.

Merton took the hint with the pistol pointed at him and stood next to Mary Fredericks.

A head appeared in the window. A face tanned by wind and sun with bright, piercing eyes.

"Your colleagues are already on their way, Superintendent," said George Cooper. He said it quietly and politely. "I stopped a car outside. The driver promised me to alert the whole of Scotland Yard. We'll have a show of force here shortly."

He climbed through the window without letting go of his walking stick and nodded amiably to Julia. Then stood in front of Merton and eyed him intently.

"So this is what a spy looks like, is it?" he said with interest. "How one can be deceived in people. What are you staring at, Merton?"

"He wants to know where you've hidden your gun," Christian said, suspecting the truth. Cooper shook his head in the manner of an old man who no longer understood the world. "Terrible people. Always thinking about firearms. It was different in my day, of course."

He lifted his walking stick and looked at it lovingly. "Beautiful piece, isn't it? Bamboo. It comes from India. And very useful. When you poke it into someone's back, it feels just like a revolver of course..."

***

Half an hour later they were sitting next to each other at the bar: With Moore, who thought tea with rum was the best remedy for a headache. Christian, who knew the prisoners were safely on their way to London. And George Cooper, who had hung the stick next to him on the bar counter.

Julia came out of the kitchen. "I'm a guest today," she said with a smile. "Tomorrow – who knows what tomorrow will bring?"

Christian stroked his aching upper arm. The police doctor had almost forced him to have the wound dressed. Now he was glad he had.

THE END